Ciaran Murtagh is a writer of books and television programmes for children. Ciaran lives in London – to find out more about what he's writing and appearing in, follow him on Twitter @ciaranmurtagh or head over to www.ciaranmurtagh.com

Books by Ciaran Murtagh

CHARLIE FLINT AND THE DINOS

Dinopants

Dinopoo

Dinoburps

Dinoball

BALTHAZAR THE GENIE

Genie in Training

Genie in Trouble

Genie in a Trap

THE FINCREDIBLE DIARY OF FIN SPENCER

Stuntboy

MEGASTAR

THE FINCREDIBLE DIARY OF FIN SPENCER

by CIARAN MURTAGH

with illustrations throughout by TIM WESSON

Piccadilly
PRESS

First published in Great Britain in 2015
by Piccadilly Press
Northburgh House, 10 Northburgh Street, London EC1V 0AT
www.piccadillypress.co.uk

A CIP catalogue record for this book is available from the British Library.

ISBN: 978-1-84812-447-9

1 3 5 7 9 10 8 6 4 2

Text design: Mina Bach
Printed and bound by Clays Ltd, St Ives Plc

Piccadilly Press is part of the Bonnier Publishing Group
www.bonnier.com

To Laura Murtagh,

the best drama teacher a kid could want!

MONDAY

My name is Fin Spencer and the last time I wrote in this diary I lied. I fibbed, told a whopper, porky-pied, you get the idea . . . Whatever you want to call it, I lied. Oops.

I didn't lie about *everything*. My name's definitely

FIN SPENCER.

It's not Neville Crumplebottom or Felicity Undercrackers or Clive Potplant or something embarrassing like that — it actually <u>is</u> Fin Spencer. I am definitely twelve years old, I do have an annoying little sister called **ELLIE** and I love ***X-WING***, the coolest rock band in the world. But I still lied.

Oh, and I <u>do</u> have a magic diary. This diary. That wasn't a lie. But you knew that right? (If not why not? Seriously, I did not stunt-jump over a shark on my bicycle for nothing!)

OK it wasn't for 'nothing', it was for a mobile phone, and the shark was clockwork, but you get my point. It was <u>**DANGEROUS**</u>, people.

Anyway, for those of you who don't know

— *seriously, what are you still doing here!?* —

this diary is magic and I'm about to prove it.

But before I do I have to say sorry for lying last time, because I promised I'd never use it again. I'm not really a diary person and when I used it loads of things went wrong. But this time I haven't got a choice. It's an emergency! A real EMERGENCY — like when you dive into a swimming pool and your shorts come off and you can't get out of the pool because everyone's watching. Oops. I've said too much. Forget about the swimming pool thing. It DID NOT happen, OK?

Besides, this emergency is much worse than that. There's a school play and a new kid in my class and everything is just wrong. If we start at the beginning you might just understand why I HAVE to use the diary ONE MORE TIME.

It's two weeks until the end of term, which, if you *have* to be at school, is the best time to be there. Nobody does any work. Not even the teachers. You just sit around chatting to your mates, playing on the computer or joining up the freckles on your best friend's face. This is my best friend, **JOSH DOYLE**. He's got more freckles than a freckle-faced freckle monster with extra freckles. If you join his freckles together you get all sorts of *cool* pictures:

Anyway, this year, instead of drawing on each other, Mrs Johnson decided we should use our 'downtime' to stage a play that she's written. It's called HOT RODS and it's the worst play in the world. It's set in olden times when there were only three TV channels and the internet hadn't been invented yet. Seriously, **NOTHING HAPPENS!**

I hate school plays. I've only been in one and it scarred me for life. It was in primary school and I was six. **JOSH** and I were playing two halves of the same donkey in the Nativity. I was the back half and **JOSH** was the front. The first two performances were fine, but in the final show everything went wrong. Josh had forgotten to go to the toilet before we got into the costume, so I spent forty-five minutes with my nose pressed up against **JOSH**'s trumping backside. I nearly died three times and I still can't breathe properly through my left nostril. In the end **JOSH** did a fart so bad I wet myself.  There were a lot of tears and a lot of wee. Mainly wee. Let's just say I NEVER WANT TO BE IN A SCHOOL PLAY AGAIN.

So when Mrs Johnson said we could do lights or sound or something if we didn't want to act I decided it'd be better if I was back*stage* rather than back*side* this time.

So that should have been fine, right?

WRONG!

There's a new kid in class called **CLIFF SHRAPNEL**. Now, in *theory* we should get on. He's just like me. He plays guitar, likes *X-WING* and makes everybody laugh. He also likes **CLAUDIA RONSON**, the prettiest girl in the school. And worse than that — she likes him back. Maybe that's the problem. **CLAUDIA** and I are supposed to be boyfriend and girlfriend. Kind of. Well, we went on a date. Once. It didn't end well.

I took her to a burger bar. But I was so

nervous, I didn't know what to say. I just sat and stared at her for fifteen whole minutes. It was awkward. Then, when she finally asked me a question I choked on my beef burger. An ambulance came. I started the date hoping to be kissed by **CLAUDIA**, I ended it being kissed by a hairy paramedic called Peter.

Let's just say there hasn't been a date two, with either **CLAUDIA** or Peter. I did think about using the diary to put it right, but I'd only just promised never to use it again. I decided to rely on my natural charm to win **CLAUDIA** back. I'm still working on it. It's only a matter of time . . . right? So if I didn't use the diary <u>then</u> you must realise how serious it is now!

Back to the school play. Mrs Johnson said that if you wanted to act in the play you had to put your name down on an audition sheet. No chance! I'd rather eat a broccoli banana. It was only as I was going home that I realised I'd made a terrible mistake. I overheard **CLAUDIA** telling her friends how much she liked actors. Then she said that as she was putting her name down on the audition sheet SHE'D SEEN CLIFF'S NAME THERE TOO.

Suddenly, I saw it all. **CLIFF** and **CLAUDIA** starring in the play together. Romance blossoming in the spotlights. A trip to a burger bar where NOBODY choked and then, before you know it, weddings, honeymoons and happily ever afters! Just like Brad and Angelina! I could <u>NOT</u> let that happen.

I raced straight back to the classroom to get my name on the audition sheet but the door was locked and Mrs Johnson had gone home. I tried to pick the lock with a paperclip, but ended up stabbing myself in the eyebrow. Mr Finch, the head teacher, walked past and said it was the first time he'd ever seen a child trying to break *into* a classroom!

THIS WAS A NIGHTMARE!

I didn't know what to do. Then I remembered the diary.

The diary could make everything better.

We all remember the diary rules, yes?

FIN SPENCER'S
FINCREDIBLE
DIARY RULES

1. The diary only changes the things I say and do or wished I'd said and done

2. It only changes things if I write about what I wish I'd done **ON THE DAY** they happen

3. Diaries are still for `losers`. It's only this one that's cool.

So everything should be fine. I've still got time to get my name on the audition sheet.

Here goes . . .

Dear diary, today I put my name down to audition for Hot Rods.

There. Audition here I come. It can't be as bad as last time, can it? There are no donkeys in HOT RODS, for one thing. In fact, that whole Nativity thing was probably just a blip. Who knows, I might even catch the acting bug and get snapped up by Hollywood. **CLAUDIA**'s got to date a guy who's won an Oscar — right?

And I've just realised that now I've started using the diary again I can use it to chronicle my inevitable rise to megastardom. That way, when I'm reclining in my gold-plated Hollywood jacuzzi, future fans can read about

how I got there. It all started with a donkey
and the need to be loved . . .

They might even make it into a movie.

TUESDAY

Have you ever been woken up by a cat licking you? I have. It happened today and it was **HORRIBLE**. It's like somebody tickling your cheek with a fish-paste toothbrush. When I opened my eyes I found the moth-eaten face of **Mr Yummy Whiskers** staring down at me. **Mr Yummy Whiskers** is my gran's cat and I'm looking after him while she's on holiday. **Mr Yummy Whiskers** hates me.

The feeling's mutual. Once I gave him a cuddle and he was sick on my head. I swear he did it on purpose. I washed my hair twenty times but it still smelled of cat food a whole week after. Every time I walked down the street, cats would chase me, licking their lips.

I'm only looking after the stupid cat because Gran's paying me twenty pounds and Mum thinks it would be good for me to 'have some responsibility'. That's mum-speak for 'I don't want to do it so you have to!'

To be honest, I'm more interested in the cash than the responsibility. There's a new **DEATH SQUADRON** game coming out next week, **DEATH SQUADRON: Apocalypse**, and I am going to be first in the class to own it thanks to Gran's dough and **Mr Yummy Whiskers**.

As if it wasn't bad enough being licked awake by a mangy moggy, when I finally woke up all I could hear was this terrible wailing. I thought **Mr Yummy Whiskers** was dying. Then I realised it was **ELLIE** singing along to her new favourite boy band, **generation cute**. **ELLIE** used to have this thing for an awful pop star called **Charlie Dimples**, but now Charlie's out of the window. Not literally, that would be terrible.

Imagine having **Charlie Dimples** hanging out of your window squawking away all the time? You'd have to move house!

The new kids on the block are **Generation Cute**. They're like **Charlie Dimples** only worse, because there are five of them and they only have one song —

'**School Dance Romance**'.

When I came out of the shower **ELLIE** was singing along to it at the top of her voice.

I went into her room to ask her to keep it down but instead she turned it up and sang right into my face.

**'You were standing
up against the wall,
You didn't notice
me at all!
I stood in front of you
and started to dance,
It was the start
of our school dance
romance!'**

Yuck! It made me want to puke up a kidney. To annoy **ELLIE** I changed some of the lyrics and sang it right back.

'You were standing
up against the wall,
You were only
two feet tall!
I stood in front of you
and started to dance,
It looked like I had
ants in my pants!
ANTS IN MY PANTS!'

Then I did a little 'ants in my pants' dance
and she threw a hairbrush at me. I ducked
and it knocked a picture off the wall. Mum
saw her do it and **ELLIE** got told off.
Result!   Maybe today wasn't going to be
so bad after all.

For breakfast I had A MASSIVE BOWL OF COCO SNAPS.

When Dad came downstairs he tried to steal them from me but when Mum saw what he was doing she told him off and gave him a slice of toast. The toast was so dry **Mr Yummy Whiskers** could have used it as a scratching post. It turns out Dad went to see the doctor yesterday and the doctor told him he had to lose some weight, so Dad's on a diet. I tried to have sympathy for him, BUT NOBODY STEALS MY COCO SNAPS AND GETS AWAY WITH IT. I made sure that every time I took a spoonful I made loads of 'Mmmmmm!'

and 'YUMMMM!' sounds just to rub it in.

When I got to school everyone was gathered around the audition sheet and my name was on the bottom. See?

I TOLD YOU THIS DIARY WAS MAGIC!

When **JOSH** saw my name he was confused.

'I thought you hated school plays,' he said. 'After what happened last time when —'

I put my hands over his mouth to make him stop speaking. Nobody needed to be reminded about the Nativity. But **CLIFF SHRAPNEL** had to ask.

What happened last time? he said.

JOSH told him — and the rest of the class — all about the farting and the donkey and how I'd choked so much I'd wet myself, and soon everyone was laughing and pointing.

Thanks, **JOSH**. Remind me why we're best friends again?

After lunch it was time for the auditions. We all went down to the school theatre and Mrs Johnson sat at a table in front of the stage like some kind of talent-show judge. Apparently we were supposed to have chosen a part and practised a speech. **I DIDN'T KNOW THAT!** I borrowed someone's script and started to read. It was worse than the PRINCESS TWINKLE CHRISTMAS SPECIAL. It was all about these hot-rod racers in olden times, and there was some

big race coming up or something and . . .
Well, I didn't get very far because I kept
getting distracted by the other auditions.
Especially when it was **JOSH**'s turn.

JOSH was auditioning for the part of
Wonky Mike, the old guy who teaches the
young guys how to race. Before **JOSH**
auditioned he went off to get changed.
When he stepped onto the stage my eyes
nearly exploded. He'd put a load of grease
in his hair, was wearing this massive leather
jacket and was walking with his auntie's
walking stick. But the WEIRDEST thing of
all was the massive beard he'd stuck to his
chin. It looked like a badger was cuddling his
chin. One or two kids started to laugh, but
Mrs Johnson shushed them and praised

Josh's 'attention to detail', which is teacher-speak for 'You look ridiculous but I'm not allowed to say so!'

When everyone had calmed down, **JOSH** started to act, or at least that's what he called it. To me he looked like a granddad at a disco. He made brumming noises as he pretended to drive around the stage. But with every 'BRUM-BRUM' he showered the front row with spit. Children were diving for cover! Then he got so carried away with all his 'BRUM-BRUM-BRUMMING' that he choked on his beard. Mrs Johnson ran onstage and ripped the beard off his face, which left an angry red mark. He looked like he'd lost an argument with a jam sandwich!

Next up was **CLAUDIA RONSON**, who didn't need any make-up or a costume to look beautiful. She was auditioning for the part of Priscilla. Priscilla's the prettiest girl in the play, so **CLAUDIA**'s perfect for it. At the end of the big race Sebastian, the coolest hot rod, gives her a kiss and they sing a song together. **CLAUDIA** has the voice of an angel and when she finished singing Mrs Johnson gave her a standing ovation.

SHE'S GOT THE PART.

CLIFF wanted the part of Sebastian. No surprise there! What did I tell you? He's trying to steal **CLAUDIA** from right under my nose! It's a good job I know what he's up to. It's obvious that I should be Sebastian. He gets all the good lines and in the end he kisses **CLAUDIA** — I mean Priscilla. The part was made for me.

CLIFF tried his best, but he's just not cool enough. It was embarrassing really. Just as he was about to sing I accidentally nudged the lighting desk and

EVERYTHING WENT DARK.

CLIFF kept on singing but it wasn't very good.

BETTER LUCK NEXT TIME, **CLIFF**.

One by one, everyone who wanted to audition had a go until finally it was my turn. Now, I'd been so distracted by all of the others that I hadn't really learned any of the lines. I didn't think that would matter. In fact, I thought if I improvised a bit it might even make the script better.

I stood on the stage and said some of the lines I could remember. Mrs Johnson didn't look very impressed so I tried out a few jokes that I'd just made up.

My hair's so old it belongs in a museum!

I'm so bored! I wish they'd invent the internet already!

I'd rather have a hot dog than a hot rod!

The kids were laughing but Mrs Johnson wasn't. She looked like she was sucking on a sea slug. What was wrong with her? Surely she could see how much I was improving her script?

When the laughter died down Mrs Johnson asked me which song I was going to sing and my heart began to pound. I'd forgotten all about the song. Suddenly I was back in the school Nativity play smelling farts, only this time they were mine. I didn't know any of the songs.

Mrs Johnson said I could sing any song at all if I wanted to, it didn't have to be from HOT RODS. **CLAUDIA** was staring at me, **CLIFF** was staring at me and **JOSH** was staring at me. In fact the whole class was staring at me. My mouth was dry and it felt like my mind had gone on holiday to Hawaii. I couldn't remember any songs at all. Not one. Zero. Zilch. Nada.

Then one popped into my head and I was so relieved I started to sing without thinking.

**'You were standing
up against the wall,
You didn't notice
me at all!'**

NOOOO!

I was singing 'SCHOOL DANCE ROMANCE'!
I was singing a GENERATION CUTE
song to my friends. It was too late to stop
now.

**'I stood in front of you
and started to dance,
It was the start
of our school dance
romance!'**

Soon the whole class was giggling. Even Mrs Johnson smiled. She winked at me and said, 'I never knew you were a fan, Fin' which is teacher-speak for 'Way to go, loser!' I was in Hot Rod Hell! Somebody kill me!

OK, so the last bit of the audition had been a

but I was sure I'd nailed the acting. If I could fix the singing mishap maybe I still had a chance. Now I know I said I was only going to use this diary for emergencies, but this IS an emergency. I **HAVE** to be in the play. My future megastardom, not to mention marriage to **CLAUDIA RONSON**, depends on it!

When I got home I knew exactly what I had to do. But before I could get to the diary I had to have dinner. Apparently, because this morning's breakfast had tempted Dad so much, we were all going to eat the same thing from now on. Besides, Mum thought it would be good for us all to get a little healthier. Mum had made something called 'Salad Surprise'.

When I asked her what the surprise was she said, 'You'll see!' Which is mum-speak for 'There isn't one'.

I was right. The only surprising thing about the salad was how much of it there was.

I munched my way through all the lettuce I could manage — **NO** lettuce! — and headed for the door. Mum reminded me that I had to feed **Mr Yummy Whiskers** before bed so I scraped the leftover salad into his bowl, ran to my bedroom and got out this diary. I need to change a few things and fast!

If I want to be Sebastian in the play then I SHOULD HAVE GOT UP EARLY THIS MORNING AND LEARNED A DIFFERENT SONG, something actually in the play! And while we're at it can we forget all about the

Nativity thing? I don't need the whole class knowing that I wet myself when I was six.

There! That should do it. Tomorrow, Fin Spencer's journey to megastardom will be back on course.

WEDNESDAY

If there's one thing worse than being woken up by a cat licking your face, it's being woken up by a cat SPITTING LETTUCE ON YOUR FOREHEAD. It turns out that Mr Yummy Whiskers doesn't like salad any more than I do. He decided to let me know by dragging half chewed bits of salad into my room and hiding them for me to find. As I pulled on my slippers I squelched a tomato.

44

Thanks, **Mr Yummy Whiskers**. Good job Gran's paying me — **DEATH SQUADRON: Apocalypse** better be worth it.

Downstairs, Mum was making breakfast, but there was no sign of my usual Coco Snaps. Instead everybody was getting scratching-post toast to be 'fair to Dad'. I tried to eat it, but it was like nibbling a porcupine's pillow. Dad could see that nobody was very happy and told us that, to make up for it, he had a surprise for us all at the weekend. He said it was somewhere 'full of adventure and discovery' and we'd all have a great time.

Result!

A new theme park —

LAND OF PERIL

— has opened on the outskirts of town

and we've been wanting to go for AGES.
Its slogan is

'*A WORLD OF ADVENTURE AND DISCOVERY*'

they say it on all the adverts. If I know Dad
like I know Dad, that's where we'll be going!
Suddenly my bristly-beard bread tasted
a lot better.

When I got to school nobody mentioned
'SCHOOL DANCE ROMANCE' so I was sure
the part of Sebastian was in the bag.
However, **BRAD RADLEY** did remember
JOSH's story about me wetting myself.
BRAD RADLEY is the meanest kid in
school — we used to be friends but it
turned out he was only pretending. I know
he remembered the pant-wetting story
because when I opened my locker I found

a big nappy in there. **BRAD** had written

'For opening night, love Brad'

across the front.

Brilliant! As if I didn't have enough to worry about.

Suddenly I was concerned. If **BRAD** remembered the wee-wee story, maybe the diary hadn't worked after all. But then I remembered, it was **JOSH** who had told everyone that story, not me, and the diary only works on things *I* say and do, so it should have worked fine for the audition song.

I got to class and the room was buzzing with excitement. Everyone wanted to know who was playing what part in the play. When Mrs Johnson arrived she was holding a golden envelope. She was really milking this talent-show judge thing. When everyone had settled down she opened the envelope, and said,

The results are in, and in no particular order the people starring in Hot Rods are . . .

Then she read out the names of everyone who had auditioned and the parts they got. **JOSH** got the part of Wonky Mike, which was no surprise really — he was the only one who had wanted it. He's still got a big red mark around his mouth from where Mrs Johnson ripped his beard off. He looks like he's been kissed by a bag of bees.

CLAUDIA got the part of Priscilla and one by one everyone else found out what parts they'd got too. Soon the only names Mrs Johnson hadn't read out were mine and **CLIFF**'s. It was between the two of us for Sebastian. Mrs Johnson looked at us and said that it had been 'a very difficult decision', which we all know is teacher-speak for 'Sorry Cliff – you are a LOSER!'

Everyone held their breath as Mrs Johnson said, 'The part of Sebastian will be played by . . . **CLIFF SHRAPNEL**!' I couldn't believe my ears! What was wrong with her? I'd made the script better *and* sung a BRILLIANT song! OK, so I hadn't actually sung a brilliant song, but the diary had made everybody believe that I had.

I'M THE MEGASTAR HERE!

CLIFF patted me on the shoulder, and said, 'Tough luck.' Which we all know is Cliff-speak for 'In your face, dweeb boy!' Mrs Johnson could see that I was upset. She said that the decision had been tough, but **CLIFF** had soldiered on in the face of 'technical difficulties' and that kind of cool head was exactly what she needed for the star of HOT RODS. Just my luck! Turning out the lights had actually *helped* **CLIFF** land the part. Then Mrs Johnson told me that it wasn't all bad news, I did still have a role.

I was going to play the part of Guy Two. I didn't even know there was a Guy <u>One</u>! I leafed through the pages looking for my lines.

I had one:

'Hey, bozo!'

THAT WAS IT!?

My starring part

was one line. How

was I going to be a

megastar with only one line, especially when

that line was 'Hey, bozo!'

WHAT IS A 'BOZO' ANYWAY?

A) A type of monkey found in Africa
B) An electric car popular in Peru
C) A Comedy sausage

Apparently, my lack of respect for the

script had given Mrs Johnson concerns.

What was she talking about?! My jokes had

actually improved her lousy play! But she had been impressed by my singing, particularly my ability to learn all fifteen verses of 'THE HOT ROD NOD' overnight. Nice one, diary! And that had given her an idea. She was giving me the most important job in the whole show.

This sounded more like it. I was born for important jobs. But as far as I could tell all of the good parts had gone. Then I had an idea. Maybe Mrs Johnson had been so impressed by my performance that she'd written a new, even better part just for me. . .

Turns out she hadn't. Mrs Johnson said I was going to be the 'understudy'. I smiled and flicked through the script to check how many lines the understudy got.

JOSH laughed and said,

The understudy gets all the lines, Fin.

I didn't understand. **JOSH** explained.

It turns out the understudy is the guy who learns **EVERY SINGLE LINE** in the play but only gets to say them when one of the real actors is sick. How rubbish is that? I have to do all of the hard work but get none of the glory! I was about to tell Mrs Johnson that I wasn't the bozo for her when she said it was understudy or nothing. It wasn't fair. I HAD TO BE IN THE PLAY! I guess I could hope that someone died. If everyone died it'd be a one-man show – **cool!**

I agreed to do it to stay close to **CLAUDIA** and **CLIFF**.

Over first break I tried to think of a way to use the diary to change things. But the auditions had been yesterday and I can only use the diary to change things on the day that they happen. And because it can't change things that other people do, IT COULDN'T CHANGE MRS JOHNSON'S DECISION. I was stuck. Who knew being a megastar would be so hard? But luckily something happened after lunch that I COULD use the diary to change. . .

When we got back to class Mrs Johnson told us we were going to spend the rest of the day on a 'Geography Field Trip', which everyone knows is teacher-speak for 'I can't be bothered to teach you. Go for a walk.'

While **JOSH** and I were looking for a pine cone we heard a scream. It was **CLAUDIA** and her friend Lucy. They were in trouble. This was just the chance I was looking for to get Claudia to notice me again.

JOSH and I ran to where the scream had come from and found **CLAUDIA** and Lisa backed into a corner. There was a spider on a leaf right in front of them and they were both pointing and shrieking. I was about to step in and rescue them, when, out of nowhere, **CLIFF SHRAPNEL** arrived, like some kind of spoddy Superman. He raced towards them, picked up the leaf and put it out of harm's way.

I couldn't believe it! That's what I was going to do!

CLAUDIA and Lucy were all giggly. **JOSH** went up and gave **CLIFF** a pat on the back and said, 'Well done, mate.' Traitor!

JOSH needs to watch it — whose best friend is he, anyway? **CLIFF** was smiling and nodding as if to say it was nothing. It **WAS** nothing!

It wasn't like he'd saved them from a radioactive poodle or something! **CLAUDIA** and Lucy asked **CLIFF** to join their team, 'in case there are any more dangers' and then the three of them went off together.

It was so unfair! That should have been me! I should have been going off with **CLAUDIA** and Lucy. **JOSH** tried to cheer me up by showing me a pine cone he'd spotted.

NOT HELPING, JOSH!

When I got home after school I tried to watch a bit of TV, but **Mr Yummy Whiskers** kept sitting on my tummy and waggling his bum in my face. It's hard to concentrate on *Distructobots* when a cat is mooning you! He was wiggling so much he accidentally

TOOK A SELFIE OF HIS BOTTOM WITH MY PHONE. I am now the proud owner of a photo of **Mr Yummy Whiskers'** bum. Just what I always wanted.

To make matters worse, **ELLIE** came back and changed the channel anyway. She had a new ꒓ENERATiON (ute doll and she wanted to watch PRiNCESS TWiNKLE'S MA꒓iC CASTLE with him. PRiNCESS TWiNKLE'S MA꒓iC CASTLE is the MOST annoying programme in the world. It turns out that the one thing that makes it even more annoying is watching it with a cat's bum in your face and a ꒓ENERATiON (ute doll going off every five seconds.

Mum had let **ELLIE** spend all her pocket money on the doll. It's called Sebastian or

Harold or someone and when you squeeze its hand it sings a bit of 'SCHOOL DANCE ROMANCE'. **ELLIE** showed me how it works, even though I wasn't interested, and **Mr Yummy Whiskers** went beserk. He loved the screeching, wailing sound the doll made and started to scratch its face with his claws. Then **ELLIE** and **Mr Yummy Whiskers** got into a tug o' war over Sebastian or Harold or whoever it was and its head came off. The doll's head, not **Mr Yummy Whiskers'** head. If **Mr Yummy Whiskers'** head came off I don't think I'd be getting my twenty pounds from Gran.

After dinner I came upstairs to practise my line for the play. It didn't take long. I tried saying 'Hey, bozo' in different accents but they all sounded stupid. This has been the worst day ever. It started with me being pelted with lettuce by an angry cat and went downhill from there. I know I'm not supposed to be using this diary unless it's an emergency, but once you start it's really hard to stop. Anyway, I've decided I might feel better if I'd rescued **CLAUDIA** from the spider. Then at least something would have gone my way today. So diary, **DO WHATEVER IT TAKES BUT LET EVERYONE THINK I SORTED OUT THAT SPIDER.** Give me a break here!

THURSDAY

This morning an **earthquake** woke me up. Seriously, the whole house was shaking and I thought I was about to die! I jumped out of bed and ran for the door only to spot Mum in the spare room doing an exercise DVD. She was jumping about and waving her arms and the floor was wobbling like a jelly bouncy castle.

Mum was the earthquake.

It looks like she's caught the health bug too. When I got back to my bedroom I noticed a funny smell. I followed my nose and found a bit of mouldy cucumber hidden behind my desk. Thank you, **Mr Yummy Whiskers**.

I found the terrible tabby asleep in my uniform drawer. He was curled up on top of my school jumper. I clapped my hands. He yelped like a princess at a pony farm and jumped three feet into the air. I smiled. It felt good to be waking <u>him</u> up for a change. When I took out my jumper, it was covered in cat hairs. I gave it a good shake but it was no use, they were properly stuck in. I pulled it on and hoped no one would notice.

Under the jumper I found Ellie's **ɡeNeRATɪᵒN CᴜᴛE** doll. **Mr Yummy**

Whiskers had dragged him up to bed with him and had licked all his hair off. Harold or Sebastian or whatever his name was looked like he was a member of a hot new boyband called ɠenᴇRᴀ⊤iᴼN ⒷⒶⓁⒹ. I gave the tiny pop star a wipe and took him downstairs. Maybe **ELLIE** wouldn't notice.

When **ELLIE** saw Harold's image change, she wasn't happy and when Mum saw my cat hair jumper she wasn't happy either. She gave me a lecture about 'taking my responsibilities seriously'. Which we all know is mum-speak for 'Keep that cat in line or you get the blame.' Despite this, and even after another breakfast of scratching-post toast, I still headed for school with a spring in my step. I was about to be treated like a hero by **CLAUDIA** for saving her from a zombie spider!

As soon as I got to school I knew something had gone <u>horribly wrong</u>. Everyone was looking at me. And not in a 'way to go, spider saviour' kind of way. More in a 'you're a monster' kind of way. I passed **CLAUDIA** and Lucy in the corridor. They both gave me the <u>nastiest</u> look EVER! **JOSH** found me by the lockers and marched me into the toilets. Apparently everyone hated me and we needed to hide until the registration bell rang.

As we cowered in a cubicle **JOSH** reminded me about what had apparently happened yesterday. I had been first on the scene when **CLAUDIA** and Lucy screamed. But instead of carefully putting the spider to one side like **CLIFF** had done, I'd jumped into the clearing, screamed 'save yourselves' at the top of my voice and pushed **CLAUDIA** and Lucy into a bush. Then I'd stamped on the spider so hard a bit of spider goo had landed on **CLAUDIA**'s dress. **CLAUDIA** had called me a **VICIOUS spider murderer** and **CLIFF** had arrived just in time to escort them chivalrously back to class.

WAY TO GO, DIARY.

When I said 'do whatever it takes' I didn't mean spider murder! I am going to have to watch what I write so much more closely . . .

When **JOSH** and I got into class everyone turned to stare at me some more. Mrs

Johnson said it was the first geography lesson she'd taught where something had actually died. Then she reminded us that we had the first reading of HOT RODS after school and everyone had to be there because we don't have long before the performances on Friday and Saturday next week. I was ready. I even knew my lines. Well, line. It's much easier when you've only got one. If she thinks I'm going to learn every other line in the play 'just in case' then she's got another think coming!

For the rest of the morning everyone gave me the cold shoulder, and **CLAUDIA** looked like she was never going to talk to me again. Luckily, I had a chance to put things right in music. There's only one electric guitar in the music room and it's usually only me who wants to play it. But now **CLIFF**'s here, he wants to play it too and it was his turn. I have to admit, **CLIFF** is a great guitarist. He's nearly as good as me. He can play a killer guitar solo without even looking at his fingers. As we watched him play, **JOSH** said we should ask him to be in a band with us. **JOSH** always wants to start a band with me. I always say no. One day I might start a band, but it won't be with **JOSH DOYLE** and it definitely won't be with **CLIFF SHRAPNEL**.

Because **CLIFF** had the guitar, I was paired with **CLAUDIA**. She still wasn't talking to me. Then I had a brainwave. Maybe I could show her that I didn't really hate spiders by writing a cute song about them!

Before long I had this nice little rhyme going:

'**You've got
eight hairy legs
and eight scary eyes,
When you appear,
girls start to cry,
But you're actually
quite nice, and
I'll tell you why,
You only hurt flies,
mister spider guy!'**

CLAUDIA started to laugh and soon
we were chatting and chuckling for the first
time in ages. It was going so well that
CLAUDIA actually suggested we go on

another date 'some time'. Which we all know is Claudia-speak for 'I want to marry you, Fin Spencer!'

Amazing!

Way to go, natural charm! I'd gone from spider murderer to hot date over the course of one music lesson.

But just as we were about to get into the details of when and where this date was going to happen, **CLAUDIA** started to sneeze. At first it was quite cute, like a hamster with the flu. But then it got worse and worse until she sounded like an elephant with a foghorn for a trunk. Then her face started to come out in nasty red blotches. Mr Burchester said it looked like she was having an allergic reaction to something. **CLAUDIA**

said she was allergic to cats. It was then that Mr Burchester spotted the hairs all over my jumper. He sent me out of the room while **CLAUDIA** recovered.

Thank you, **Mr Yummy Whiskers!** The love of my life is allergic to me. Well, to my jumper, at least. **CLAUDIA** was sent home in the end. So now she hates me because I bring her out in hives **AND** because I'm a spider murderer. I just wanted the day to end so I could go home. But as I was heading for the door Mrs Johnson stopped me — had I forgotten about the read-through this evening?

It turns out I had.

No biggie. I only had one line. How hard could it be?

Very, it turns out. Because **CLAUDIA** had been sent home I had more than one line. I had all of her lines too! As if it wasn't bad enough PRETENDING TO BE A GIRL IN FRONT OF THE WHOLE CLASS, right at the end of the play I had to do a scene with **CLIFF** where I had to big him up and say all sorts of cringey things like:

You're awesome

and

Way to go, superstar

and

Whenever I'm around you, I feel like I'm walking on stardust!

It was that last one that got the whole class laughing. We were just coming up to the big kiss when Mrs Johnson decided to call the rehearsal to an end! **Thank goodness!** As we were leaving Mrs Johnson said that she hoped **CLAUDIA** was feeling better tomorrow. Me too!

Don't worry, Miss, SHE WILL BE. I'm going to get the diary to make sure of it.

It had been such a terrible day that when I got home I needed some chocolate. I went to the secret chocolate stash in the kitchen only to find it had all been thrown out.

Mum told me it was 'unfair on Dad to have chocolate in the house.' Which we all know is mum-speak for 'Dad's a fatty who can't control himself. No more chocolate ever.'

I came upstairs to write this. I can't change the spider thing — that happened yesterday — but I can at least try to make sure **CLAUDIA** didn't have an allergic reaction to my hairy jumper. If we hadn't sat next to each other in music none of this would have happened. She would still have the pretty face she was born with and I wouldn't have had to be lovey-dovey with **CLIFF** in the HOT RODS rehearsal.

COME ON, DIARY. MAKE IT HAPPEN.

FRIDAY

When I got to school today I was still a spider murderer and **CLAUDIA** still wasn't talking to me, but nobody remembered anything about an allergic reaction or about me telling **CLIFF** I walked on stardust whenever he was around.   Result!   I'd even remembered to wash my jumper and shut my clothes drawer last night, so there was no repeat of the **Mr Yummy Whiskers** incident.   Double result!

Unfortunately, though, because **CLAUDIA** didn't sit next to me in music yesterday, I didn't write the spider song and she didn't remember anything about the date we were supposed to be going on —

DISASTER!

It might take forever to get her to ask me again . . .

During first break **JOSH** tried to cheer me up with a computer game magazine he'd bought. It was all about **DEATH SQUADRON: APOCALYPSE**. It looked amazing. Apparently there's more brains, blood and burst body bits than ever. I just _have_ to play it. **JOSH** and I are going to be first in the queue next

Sunday and then the race is on to see who can finish it quickest. **JOSH** thinks it'll be him, but he doesn't stand a chance. I've been a **DEATH SQUADRON** champion for six months' running. OK, maybe not running. There was that little blip when my sister suddenly got really good thanks to my diary, but that didn't last long once I'd put a stop to it.

At break time everybody was standing by the school noticeboard laughing. I went to see what the joke was. Apparently I was the joke! **BRAD RADLEY** had made a poster and stuck it to the noticeboard at break time. It said: Wanted for Spider Murder! Fin Spencer! And there was a picture of me holding a machine gun and splatting a load of spiders. Thanks, **BRAD**.

After school we had another rehearsal for HOT RODS. Now that we'd had the read-through, Mrs Johnson wanted us to practise a couple of the songs. Because the diary made it seem like I'd learned all the words to 'THE HOT ROD NOD' for the audition she asked me to teach the song to everyone while she played the piano. 'THE HOT ROD NOD' is fifteen lines long and every single line sounds the same.

**'Hot Rod!
The screech
of the tyres!
Hot Rod!
Race down
to the wire!'**

By the time I got to line fourteen and fifteen I was just making it up.

Hot Rod!
Fastest guy wins!
Hot Rod!
Turn left at the bins!
Hot Rod!
Try not to crash!
Hot Rod!
We eat bangers and mash!

Nobody noticed. They were so bored they just sang along to whatever I said and Mrs Johnson was too busy concentrating on playing the piano to listen. She's written the songs and music herself and **THEY'RE TERRIBLE.** They're from the olden times when everybody had quiffs and nobody rapped. It would have been better if we'd used some **X-WING** songs. To be honest, it would have been better if we'd used some Generation Cute songs!

To finish the show there's a love duet between Sebastian and Priscilla called 'You and Me Always'. It's soppier than a puppy in a Santa costume but, right at the end of the song, Sebastian and Priscilla kiss. I could not let that happen! Yesterday **CLAUDIA** had asked me out on a date and now she was about to kiss **CLIFF SHRAPNEL** live on stage in front of me? No way!

As **CLIFF** and **CLAUDIA** got to the end of the song I pretended to have a coughing fit. I was kicking my legs and banging the floor and making so much noise that Mrs Johnson stopped playing and came to help. She thumped my back so hard I thought she was trying to turn me into a puppet.

When I finished coughing, the song and the kiss had been forgotten — RESULT! Mrs Johnson decided it was time to call the rehearsal to an end and reminded us to learn our lines over the weekend. Easy! I only have one line and I've already learned it. Then she reminded me that BECAUSE I WAS UNDERSTUDY I HAD TO LEARN EVERY LINE IN THE PLAY. She knew it wouldn't be a problem as I obviously had a head for memorising words. Thank you, Mrs Johnson. Way to ruin a weekend.

When I got home Mum had made a soup out of all the salad I hadn't been eating. It looked like pond water. It tasted worse. Luckily tomorrow we're going on Dad's surprise visit to LAND OF PERIL so there'll be hot dogs and burgers aplenty! I can starve until then. After dinner I looked up LAND OF PERIL on the computer and tried to decide which ride I'd go on first — the Splashanator or the Polorizer? The decision was obvious — GET WET ON THE SPLASHANATOR AND THEN DRY YOURSELF ON THE POLORIZER.

Friday night is movie night in our house. We take it in turns to pick a film and we all have to watch it. I always pick something cool like ZOMBIE HEAD SPLAT or REVENGE OF THE CYBORG PETROL PUMP. Tonight it was **ELLIE**'s turn and she picked PRINCESS TWINKLE'S MAGIC CASTLE: THE MOVIE.

She's picked PRINCESS TWINKLE'S MAGIC CASTLE: THE MOVIE for her last *seven* movie nights. We keep trying to persuade her to try something else but she never does.

PRINCESS TWINKLE'S MAGIC CASTLE: THE MOVIE is so bad I'd rather watch **JOSH DOYLE** dance flamenco in a frilly dress.

By halfway through I wanted to pull my eyes out through my nose. By three-quarters of the way through I wanted to pull **ELLIE**'s eyes out through her nose. Even **Mr Yummy Whiskers** looked like he hated it. He decided he'd rather count the hairs on his own tail than watch another minute! Normally, these nights are made better by popcorn and sweets, but because of Dad's diet we had to eat celery.

By the time the credits rolled, Dad was asleep, Mum was doing the ironing and my brain felt like it had turned into a cheese triangle. As **ELLIE** headed up to bed I saw that she'd left her ꒱ENERATION CUTE doll on the sofa. To get a little bit of revenge I decided to hide it under the armchair.

As I was getting into my pyjamas, Mum stopped me and called me into her bedroom. Like some kind of super spy, she handed over a package. It was from Gran. Inside was a postcard thanking me for taking such good care of Mr Yummy Whiskers and a big pack of CHOCOLATE. Despite the whole family health kick, Mum thought I should have the chocolate because I'm doing such a good job with Mr Yummy Whiskers. She said as long as I keep it hidden from Dad it's all mine. Like that's a problem! I always keep my chocolate hidden from Dad whether I'm supposed to or not!

As I hid the chocolate in my wardrobe I found a partly sucked lettuce leaf in my trainer. THANK YOU, Mr Yummy Whiskers.

I tried to think of a way to use the diary to make things just a little better. But the movie choice was **ELLIE**'s and there was nothing I could do about **BRAD** so I've just got to suck it up! Never mind! I know tomorrow is going to be brilliant! LAND OF PERIL, here we come!

SATURDAY

Today things did not go according to plan. You would never guess where I'm writing this diary from. Let's just say it's not LAND OF PERIL, more like Land of EVIL. **WHAT WAS DAD THINKING?**

The day started fine. When I woke up I was raring to go. It's not every day you get to visit the coolest theme park in the country. Turns out that, for me, it wasn't going to be

today, either.
When I got
downstairs,
Dad had this
big smile on
his face. He
looked like he'd

won the Lottery, the
World Cup and Mr Universe all in one go.
He'd got something really cool to tell us and
I knew exactly what it was!

Breakfast was more scratching-post
toast, which to be honest was better than
pond-water soup, but I'm starving! The
LAND OF PERIL burger bar can not
come soon enough. After breakfast Dad told
us his surprise.

'This weekend,' he says, 'we are going to visit . . .' and I'm ready to hear the words LAND OF PERIL. But that's not what he says. Instead he says

Rainbow Grove

I can't believe my ears. What's **Rainbow Grove**?? For a minute I decide to give Dad the benefit of the doubt. Maybe **Rainbow Grove** is an even <u>cooler</u> theme park that's just opened and is so new I haven't even heard of it yet! It sounds worryingly like a PRINCESS TWINKLE kind of place, but it might be OK. Turns out it was **NOT** OK.

Dad hands over the brochure for me to

look at and my heart drops. **Rainbow Grove** isn't a theme park, not even a rubbish one. It's some kind of weird prison for adults, or at least that's what it looked like. It was a '**Health and Wellbeing Centre**' whatever that is. The brochure was full of photos of people planting crops, eating brown food and sitting in a circle crying. I knew how they felt. If I had to live there I'd cry too.

Dad explains that it's all part of his healthy living kick. You can live at **Rainbow Grove** if you want . . .

My blood runs cold. We're not going to move in to **Rainbow Grove**, are we? But then Dad finishes his sentence. Or you can visit for a weekend. That's what we're doing. For a moment I'm relieved that we're not actually going to be living there, but then I remember we're not going to LAND OF PERIL either and I'm angry again. I clicked through some of the pages: there were bike rides, healthy food, earth-chanting, aura-channelling and the chance to 'be at one with nature', whatever that meant. It sounded suspiciously like a geography field trip to me.

Mum smiled and said, 'What a lovely surprise.' Which we all know is mum-speak for 'I hate surprises!' And she sent us all off to pack.

While we're packing I try to persuade Mum that I should be allowed to stay behind and look after Mr Yummy Whiskers. I don't want to be at one with nature. I tried it once this week and I ended up killing a spider! Mum isn't having any of it. Apparently I'm 'too young to be left on my own.' Which we all know is mum-speak for 'If I'm going, you're coming with me.' I ask if we can bring **Mr Yummy Whiskers**, but the brochure says 'no pets'. Mum thinks he'll be all right for one night so I start packing.

WHAT DO YOU PACK FOR A TRIP TO A HEALTH AND WELLBEING CENTRE?

Incense?
Sandals?
A dream catcher?

TRICK QUESTION! IT'S ALL THREE!!

I throw in some jeans and a T-shirt but there's still loads of room in my bag. I add the diary, just in case. Then I have an idea. I unplug my

Xbox and shove that in too. I hide it under my jeans. While everyone else is being 'at one with nature' maybe I can be 'at one' with **DEATH SQUADRON**. I briefly consider trying to pack the portable TV, but there wouldn't really be enough room in my bag and besides, everywhere has a TV, right? It's not like **Rainbow Grove** won't have one. . .

I drag my bag downstairs and leave it in the hall. Mum tells me to leave out two days of cat food and make sure the cat flap is open for **Mr Yummy Whiskers**. I am about to do just that when Dad calls me to help him load the car. Seriously! Parents need to coordinate their instructions! **I ONLY HAVE ONE PAIR OF HANDS, PEOPLE!**

As I'm loading the car **ELLIE** stops me. She can't find her ƃᴇNᴇʀᴀᴛⁱᴼN ᴄᵘᵗᵉ doll and wants me to help her find it. I'm about to tell her where I've hidden it when Dad tells me off for not loading the car! I can't believe this. Now three people want me to do jobs and none of them are happy! **DON'T THEY KNOW IT'S A SATURDAY?** I'm supposed to be on the sofa!

The trip to **Rainbow Grove** takes all morning. To make matters worse we went right past LAND OF PERIL. As we drove by I stuck my nose against the window and dreamed of what might have been. For a moment I thought about grabbing the steering wheel and making Dad drive the car straight onto the Polorizor.

Even if we ended up in prison it would be more fun than **Rainbow Grove**.

When we finally got to **Rainbow Grove** a bearded guy in a tie-dye shirt and sandals was waiting for us. I can't take my eyes off his toenails. They're so long that when he dances he probably stabs himself in the eye! He's called Lucas and he runs the place. Before we go in he shows us a list of rules.

Rainbow Grove
RULES

1. Be happy
2. Be yourself
3. No 'naughty' food
4. No phones or other electrical equipment
5. Be yourself
6. Be happy

I point out that he's written two of the rules twice. He says that's because **"be yourself and be happy"** are the most important rules there are. I ask him whether that means we are allowed electrical equipment because without it I won't be very happy. Lucas ruffles my hair and says, 'What a cutie.' Which we all know is Hippy-speak for 'Shut up, kid'.

Mum and Dad hand over their phones and keys and I decide to keep quiet about the games console in my bag — I hoped I'd be able to find a TV room or something and sneak in a game when no one was watching.

Lucas led us to the dormitories. That's right: DORMITORIES. The girls sleep in one room and the boys sleep in another. Dad and I make our way to the boy's dormitory. It is full of bunk beds and smells like an elephants' fart jar.

FART

Dad lets me take the top bunk and as we unpack he smiles and says, 'It won't be that bad!' Which we all know is dad-speak for 'Strap in, kid, this could get rough!'

Once we're unpacked we've got time for one afternoon activity before dinner. Lucas shows us a list:

Rainbow Grove
ACTIVITIES

- Laughter therapy
- Tantric drumming
- Panpipe whittling
- Aura-channelling
- Cycling with your chakra

The only one that sounds vaguely normal is the cycling, so Dad, **ELLIE** and me choose that while Mum goes to channel her aura, whatever that means...

Lucas gives Dad a map and a compass — has he never heard of a satnav? — and sends us on our way. Soon we're completely lost. **ELLIE** starts to cry and Dad is trying to read the map upside down. He isn't getting very far. I offer some helpful instructions and then he gets angry and gives the whole thing to me because 'I'm such an expert', apparently. I look at the map. I HAVE NO IDEA WHERE WE ARE. I see a squiggly line that I think is a stream, then I spot a stream on the other side of the field so we head for that. If we follow the stream we should get right back to **Rainbow Grove**. (Although why we would want to get back to **Rainbow Grove** I'm still not sure!)

It turns out that the squiggly line on the map wasn't a stream. We end up on a motorway and suddenly **ELLIE** is crying louder than ever and Dad is trying to dodge lorries. I hope Mum is having more fun than us. To be honest, she couldn't be having less.

When the police find us it's dark and everybody is tired. The police give us a lift back to **Rainbow Grove** and **ELLIE** and Dad aren't talking to me. Apparently this is all my fault! It's so unfair. If it's anybody's fault it's Dad's! If he'd taken us to LAND OF PERIL in the first place then we wouldn't be in this situation.

When we get inside, Mum tells us we've missed dinner but she's saved us some. **SHE REALLY SHOULDN'T HAVE.** I poke at a plate of leftover lentils and sprouting beans and ask if there's anything else. Lucas overhears and comes back with a wheatgrass smoothie. I <u>HAD</u> to ask.

With nothing else to do I decide to head to bed. I try to get to sleep, but everyone's snoring and shuffling and it's cold and I'm starving. I take out the diary to make sure I don't forget how bad all of this has been. My tummy rumbles for the hundreth time and I remember the chocolate Gran sent me from Tenerife. It's sitting in my bedroom waiting for me and I'd do anything to have it right here now.

Then I realise I **CAN** do anything. If I'd packed the chocolate in my suitcase this morning then I wouldn't be hungry. Even better, if I'd packed my portable TV then I could be playing **DEATH SQUADRON** while I munched. I know I won't remember any of it, but at least I won't wake up hungry. I'm going to go straight to bed so the diary can work its magic. With any luck there'll be some chocolate left over for tomorrow too!

SUNDAY

If the first and most important rule of **Rainbow Grove Health and Wellbeing Centre** was to BE HAPPY then as soon as I woke up I could tell Lucas had broken it. From his terrifying toenails right up to his silly ponytail, Lucas was a very angry man. Looking around it didn't take me long to figure out why. My top bunk was covered in chocolate wrappers and there was a big brown stain on the pillow where I'd dribbled in my sleep.

It turns out the diary had worked its magic and I had stuffed my face with chocolate last night. What's more, I had apparently woken the whole dorm by shouting

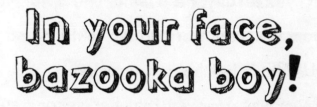

at the top of my voice. I must have been playing a very exciting game of **DEATH SQUADRON**. I couldn't remember it of course, but I had to laugh when Lucas told me. This made him even angrier, which I thought was strange when he wanted everyone to be happy!

We were all marched into Lucas's office and told we were being thrown out of **Rainbow Grove**. Apparently I'd broken the two most important rules of the centre at the same time — no electronics and no naughty food! I tried to point out to Lucas that yesterday he'd said the two most important rules were to BE HAPPY and BE YOURSELF, but he just growled.

Mum was annoyed that her second aura-channelling session had to be cancelled, **ELLIE** seemed over the moon that I was getting in trouble and Dad was really embarrassed by the whole thing. Dad's embarrassment quickly turned to anger when Lucas revealed **Rainbow Grove**'s Rule Seven:

⊘ 7. No refunds

We climbed back in the car and set off home. If the journey had taken ages yesterday, today it went on FOREVER. We got stuck in a traffic jam on the motorway. Mum tried to lighten the mood by playing 'eye spy' but it's amazing how quickly you run out of things to spy when you haven't moved for two hours.

At the service station Dad insisted we should still try to have a healthy weekend and order the 'healthy option' for lunch. Which is dad-speak for 'a cheap sandwich'. I didn't even know what was in mine. I was too scared to ask. It tasted like it could be:

1.   Belly button jelly
2.   Toe juice paste
3.   Ear wax spread

It might even have been a combination of all three. Dad hadn't said a word to me all journey and I thought I could get back in his good books by giving him some of the leftover chocolate I still had in my bag. Mum caught me as I was handing it over and confiscated the lot. It was so unfair! Sometimes I think it's impossible to make both of your parents happy at the same time! I'm surprised I even bother to try.

Unfortunately the worst was yet to come . . .

When we finally got home the place looked like a bomb had hit it. Seriously, it looked like a hurricane had had a party with a tornado and decided to invite a hailstorm along for good measure. Mum thought we'd been burgled.

Dad thought there had been an earthquake. No one knew for sure what had happened.

Turns out **Mr Yummy Whiskers** had happened. He was sitting in the middle of the living room swishing his tail with a big smile on his face.

In my rush to please EVERYBODY yesterday I'd forgotten to open the cat flap or leave out any food and in revenge **Mr Yummy Whiskers** had created kitty carnage.

He'd shredded the curtains, ripped the sofa and somehow smashed the lampshade. How had he even got up there?

1 STILTS?
2 BUNGEE ROPE?
3 HOVER BOOTS?

Mr Yummy Whiskers must be some kind of flying cat or something. Or maybe he has a secret spy kit stashed away that he keeps for special occasions . . .

The only good news was that **ELLIE** had found her ꭲENERATɪᵒN Cʊте doll. Unfortunately, **Mr Yummy Whiskers** had found it first and turned it into a chew toy.

Mr Yummy Whiskers had also managed to poo in every room in the house, which was impressive considering I hadn't left him any cat food! What was even more impressive was that every poo was different.

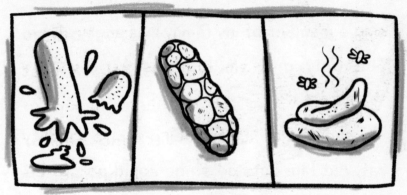

A Pictorial Guide to Types of Cat Poo by Fin Spencer, Esq.

One was brown and squelchy, another was white and hard and another was so smelly it made my nose bleed.

Somehow all of this was my fault. Mum made me go around every room with a cloth and spray and clean up the poo. Then I had to get my money box and give **ELLIE** all the money I'd been saving towards **DEATH SQUAD: APOCALYPSE** so that she could buy a new ɢENERATiᵒN CUTE doll. By bedtime I smelled of cat poo, had no money and every single member of my family was angry at me. The only one smiling was **Mr Yummy Whiskers.**

I shouted at him for being such a naughty cat, put him outside so he could poo to his heart's content, locked the cat flap and came up to bed.

As I've been writing I've been trying to think of a way the diary can help me fix all of this. But it's impossible. The whole **Mr Yummy Whiskers** thing happened yesterday and quite frankly I was pleased to be out of **Rainbow Grove** so I didn't want to fix that! What's the point in having a magic diary if it's so USELESS!

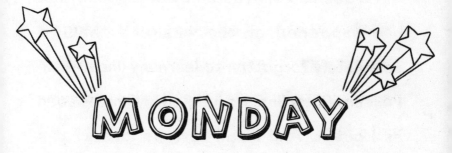

MONDAY

Today started badly and got worse. Dad was still angry about the whole **Rainbow Grove** thing so decided to ban chocolate from the house altogether. Because I'd tried to be nice and share some with him, he knew about my secret stash and confiscated it. He said he'd put it in a 'safe place', which we all know is dad-speak for 'my stomach'. This week was going to be a disaster, I could feel it in my bones. As if I didn't have enough to worry about with the play coming up.

I'd been so distracted by everything that had happened at the weekend that I'd completely forgotten to learn my lines. Well, I'd learned *my* line. I'd learned my line as soon as I got it. And I still have no idea what a bozo is:

WHAT IS A BOZO?

A) A rotten banana
B) A Chinese panda
C) A novelty bow tie

What I hadn't learned were **ALL OF THE OTHER LINES IN THE PLAY.** As far as I was concerned it was a waste of time. It was as pointless as being nice to a stingy relative

— you're never going to get the five-pound note in your birthday card, so why bother? As long as nobody got ill I was never going to have to say any of those lines and Mrs Johnson would never know I hadn't learned them.

When I got to school **JOSH** and **CLIFF** were chatting by the lockers. I did not like the look of that. It turned out I was right to be suspicious. **JOSH** and **CLIFF** had spent the whole weekend together. They'd even formed a band with the lousiest name in the history of lousy names: SYSTEM OF THE FUTURE. System of the Future is not a cool band name. That's why **JOSH** needs me as a best friend. I'm always coming up with cool band names — Macramé, Cloud Pirates, The

Chocolate Toast Machine. I'm full of them. Cool band names flow from me like snot from a toddler.

Anyway, the name of the band wasn't the point. The fact that the band existed was the point! What was **JOSH DOYLE** thinking? Whose best friend was he, anyway? And what was **CLIFF SHRAPNEL** playing at? First he'd taken my girlfriend, then he'd taken my part in the play and now he was taking my best friend. HE MUST BE STOPPED!

JOSH didn't see what the big deal was. He wouldn't! He's still got an angry rash from wearing that comedy beard. His mouth looks like a baboon's bottom. **CLIFF** agreed with Josh. He said there was room for me in his band if I wanted to join.

Wait! Did I just hear right? His band!? HIS BAND!? I wouldn't join 'his' band if it was the last band on the planet and they had a million-pound recording deal. (OK, I might join then, but <u>ONLY</u> then!) If I'm going to join anyone's band it will be my own band, thank you very much. **CLIFF SHRAPNEL** is stealing my life bit by bit. And as for Josh, well, who needs a best friend like that? **CLIFF** is welcome to the baboon-bum-mouthed bumble-head. I left the two new BFFs to it and went to class.

In history we were asked to make a castle out of bits of junk Mr Moore had brought in. **JOSH** and **CLIFF** decided to work together, or rather **CLIFF** bossed **JOSH** about while he did none of the work. I couldn't believe it!

Ordering **JOSH DOYLE** around used to be MY job!

I didn't mind much — I could make a castle on my own. Besides, nobody took these things seriously — it was nearly the end of term and this was just a time-wasting exercise.

It turns out nobody takes these things seriously unless your name is **CLIFF SHRAPNEL**. He and **JOSH** made this amazing castle with yoghurt-pot turrets and a lollipop-stick drawbridge. It looked like something out of a fairy tale. Mine looked like something out of a nightmare. To be honest, I hadn't really tried. I'd just folded a couple of bits of paper together and put up a toothpick flagpole. If a king was unlucky enough to live in it he'd be King Dweeb of Loserville.

Everyone went to have a look at **CLIFF**
and **JOSH**'s castle and soon they were the
centre of attention. Nobody even bothered
to glance at mine. That was the final straw.
CLIFF had taken my whole life. Worse
than that, he was the cool version of me
that everyone liked. Just because he was
new at school everyone was being super nice
to him. Then Mr Moore suggested that

CLIFF's castle might be even better with a moat so he and the whole class went off with little plastic cups to get water from the toilets. I didn't go! If **CLIFF** wants a moat he can get it himself! I am not **CLIFF SHRAPNEL**'s slave. That's **JOSH DOYLE**'s job.

For a moment I was left alone with the castle. I walked over to have a look. I had to admit it was pretty good. The yoghurt-pot turrets were a great idea. I picked it up to have a closer look just as **JOSH** came back into the room.

WHAT ARE YOU DOING?

he yelled.

I hadn't heard him come in so he made me jump. AND I LET GO OF THE CASTLE. I watched, in slow motion, as it flew into the air. The rest of the class and Mr Moore came back just in time to see it smash in pieces on the floor. Mr Moore dropped his little cup of water.

Fin Spencer!

he shouted.

What have you done?

Which we all know is teacher-speak for 'Prepare to die, dweeb boy.' I tried to explain that it was all Josh's fault, which it kind of was, but he wasn't listening. **JOSH**

didn't help. He kept saying that he was nowhere near the castle when it got smashed so how could it be his fault? Because everyone knew that I didn't get on with **CLIFF**, and I'd been the only kid in the class not to go and get water for the moat, they all presumed I'd done it on purpose.

Mr Moore said 'drastic action' needed to be taken. Which we all know is teacher-speak for 'Seriously, prepare to die, dweeb boy.'

I knew I was in trouble, but I had no idea how much. Mr Moore sent me to see Mr Finch the headmaster. I tried to explain to him what had happened, but the more I explained the worse it sounded. He called for Mrs Johnson because she's my form teacher and when she heard what had happened she kicked me out of the play as punishment! I AM NO LONGER GUY TWO IN HOT RODS. I couldn't believe it! I mean, I didn't want to be in the play in the first place, but now that I was I didn't want to be kicked out of it either. I did all I could to persuade her to give me a second chance, but she wasn't listening. I told her nobody could say 'Hey bozo!' like me and to prove it I showed her all of my accents:

1 Mexican
2 Irish
3 Bulgarian
4 Another Mexican

She shook her head. She said being in HOT RODS was all about being part of a team and

I clearly wasn't a team player. Mr Finch agreed. They sent me back to the history department to tidy up the mess while the rest of my class went to practise the dance moves for the play.

Once I'd finished sweeping I found them all in the theatre. I wasn't allowed to join in so I sat on a chair at the back to watch. IT WASN'T FAIR! Dancing was the one thing I would have been good at — I have some killer moves. Well, my moves can kill people, which is practically the same thing.

Just when I thought things couldn't get any worse, **CLIFF** started to show off some of his body-popping — is there nothing this kid can't do? Then **JOSH** threw away his walking stick and started to copy him. Mrs Johnson thought this was so hilarious that she wrote it into the script. Can you believe that? In my audition I improved the whole play, but I only got made Guy Two. **CLIFF** invents a stupid dance sequence and it gets put in the play.

After school Mum takes **ELLIE** and me to the shops so that **ELLIE** can buy herself a new ᏀᎬ N ᎬRATioN ᏟuᎢᎬ doll with my money! When we get to the shops it turns out the dolls are on offer, two for the price of one. So instead of buying one doll with my money she gets to buy two.

If you squeeze their hands at the same time they sing in harmony. All the way home in the car **ELLIE** squeezed their hands again and again and again. It was like being trapped in a car with two choking chinchillas.

When we finally got home **Mr Yummy Whiskers'** food is untouched in his bowl. Nobody's seen him all day. I checked the cat flap was open and had a look in the garden but I'm not that worried — it means **ELLIE**'s dolls are safe for the night and I won't get slapped in the face with a lettuce leaf tomorrow morning. Anyway, I've got more important things to think about.

DIARY, YOU NEED TO FIX THIS.

I can't not be in the play. I know I don't have many lines, but I can't let **CLIFF** and **CLAUDIA** be all romantic without being there to stop them. Besides, I didn't mean to drop the castle. I really didn't. Sure, I don't like **CLIFF** very much but I wouldn't stamp on a guy's castle for that. So, diary, fix it so that I didn't touch **CLIFF**'s castle today. I didn't even pick it up to have a look. When I'm a megastar I'll thank you in my Oscar speech.

TUESDAY

This morning I overslept. I woke up and it was already eight-thirty — WHERE WAS **MR YUMMY WHISKERS** WHEN YOU NEEDED HIM? Who thought anyone would ever need **Mr Yummy Whiskers**?! I raced downstairs and out of the door without even stopping for breakfast, which is probably just as well as I don't think I could face another slice of **throat-ripper toast.**

When I got to school I knew the diary had worked. **CLIFF**'s castle was sitting in reception looking as good as new. Whenever a student does a really good piece of work Mr Finch puts it in reception. It doesn't even have to be that good. **JOSH** once drew a picture of Mr Finch that made him look like Mr Bean. It still got put in reception. With **CLIFF**'s castle in reception I was back in the play and back on course for megastardom.

RESULT!

In class Mrs Johnson made everyone give **CLIFF** a clap for doing such a 'great piece of art'. Which we all know is teacher-speak for 'being the world's biggest creep.' She even gave him three merits. I tried not to be too angry. I guess it was a small price to pay for still being Guy Two in HOT RODS. As we were heading to science, **JOSH** and **CLIFF** asked if I wanted to rehearse with their band at lunchtime. Can't these guys take a hint? Fin Spencer is a solo star! If he's going to be in a band it will be his band, not anybody else's!

In science I was still angry with **JOSH** about the whole band thing. What kind of friend goes behind his best friend's back like that? I was so busy fuming that I didn't really hear the instructions that Mr Lilley gave for the science experiment. It was something to do with green crystals and blue liquid or blue crystals and green liquid — I couldn't remember which. He could see that I hadn't been listening and asked, 'Have you got that, Fin?' Which we all know is teacher-speak for 'Admit you weren't listening and die!' Did he think I'd fall for that?

So I nod and say, 'Got it!' Which we all know is Fin-speak for 'I'll figure it out!' How hard can it be?

TURNS OUT, VERY HARD.

The green liquid and the blue liquid looked identical and I couldn't tell which was which. I just picked the coolest-looking one and added some of the nearest crystals.

BOOM!

I flew off my workbench and landed on the floor. The science lab filled with smoke and the fire alarms went off. Mr Lilley opened the fire escape and we all had to stand in the rain for twenty minutes until the smoke cleared. Mr Lilley was very angry and gave me a red docket to go and see Mr Finch after school. When we got back inside **JOSH** asked me what had happened to my eyebrows. **JOSH** can ask some very weird questions sometimes so I thought nothing of it. Then **CLIFF** asked the same question. Were they both trying to trick me? <u>WHAT DID THEY MEAN?</u> My eyebrows were on my forehead like they always were, weren't they?

Apparently they weren't. The explosion had blown my eyebrows completely off.

When science finished **JOSH** took me to the toilets so I could see for myself. I looked like a confused marmoset! What was I going to do? I couldn't

spend the rest of the day like that. **JOSH** said that he had an idea. When **JOSH** says he has an idea I normally run a mile. He never has a *good* idea, it's always just *an* idea. But I was desperate so I let him get on with it.

He took out a black marker and coloured in where my eyebrows used to be. The problem was he wasn't very good at colouring and my forehead was quite sore so I kept twitching. By the time **JOSH** had finished I had two big thick eyebrows drawn on my forehead and I looked like a DIY Dracula. Seriously, my eyebrows were bushier than a meercat's moustache! I tried to wipe off some of the ink, but JOSH had done it in permanent marker. He couldn't understand why I was angry. I pointed to my marker pen eyebrows. This is why I'm angry — I've got a Sharpie monobrow! It was the final straw. I told him that perhaps he'd be better off being friends with CLIFF from now on because our friendship was not working. JOSH said he was 'only trying to help' which is Josh-speak for 'make things worse'. I'd heard enough and went to get some lunch.

I spent the rest of the day trying to keep out of sight. I didn't want anyone to see what

134

had happened to my face. I found an old baseball cap in my locker and wore it low over my forehead. Luckily we had rehearsals for the rest of the afternoon and I told Mrs Johnson that the cap was me getting into character, like **JOSH** with the beard. Mrs Johnson smiled and said that it was good to see me taking my role seriously for a change.

The only good thing about the whole play happens right in the middle. **GUY TWO HAS A FIGHT WITH SEBASTIAN.** Today we were rehearsing that. Mrs Johnson taught us how to throw punches so it looked like we were hitting each other when really we weren't. I thought it would be much easier if we just hit each other but Mrs Johnson didn't like that idea. For thirty marvellous minutes I pretended to punch **CLIFF** up and down the stage while shouting 'Hey, bozo!' at the top of my voice. I think I could get used to megastardom! Mrs Johnson said it all looked 'very convincing'! You don't know the half of it, Miss!

After the rehearsal I overheard **CLAUDIA** talking to her friends. **JOSH**'s rash had finally cleared up so he had put his beard back on and she thought it made him look handsome. I nearly swallowed my own head! Seriously! **JOSH DOYLE**? Handsome? I suppose anything that covered up half his face was an improvement, but still! Between **JOSH** and his beard and **CLIFF** with his cool part in HOT RODS, what chance did I have of getting **CLAUDIA** to notice me?

Just as I was thinking that, **CLAUDIA** did notice me. Unfortunately she noticed my ridiculous eyebrows. Before she could say anything I pulled my cap down over my forehead and headed for the door. But as I was about to leave Mr Finch stopped me. He'd heard all about the incident in the science lab and didn't I have a red docket? I'd forgotten all about that. Suddenly all of the fun I'd had pretending to punch **CLIFF** evaporated. It was time to go and sit in Mr Finch's office for a lecture.

Before he started, Finch told me to take the cap off — it wasn't proper school uniform. I tried to tell him that my Sharpie eyebrows weren't proper school uniform either but he wasn't listening. When he saw what **JOSH** had done he tried to be all serious and stern but I could tell that he was trying not to laugh. He said that perhaps my new eyebrows would serve as a reminder to me not to mess about in science, and then he sent me home.

When I got home I kept the cap on. I didn't need anyone else asking questions. Unfortunately **ELLIE** could tell something was up and kept on asking why I was wearing the hat. Luckily no one was really paying much attention to **ELLIE**. Mum and Dad were too distracted: **MR YUMMY WHISKERS** WAS OFFICIALLY MISSING. Nobody had seen him since Sunday. Mum thought I probably shouted at him a little bit too loudly after what had happened with the poo and things and that he had run away.

<u>BRILLIANT!</u> Apparently this was <u>all my</u> <u>fault again.</u> I didn't tell them about locking the cat flap. If they thought it was my fault already they'd definitely think it was my fault then! Which it kind of was, I suppose, although really it was Dad's for taking us to **Rainbow Grove** in the first place. Mum helpfully pointed out that Gran would kill me if **Mr Yummy Whiskers** wasn't back by the time she got home from Tenerife so I had better find him. She was right, but I knew it was worse than that. If **Mr Yummy Whiskers** didn't come back I wouldn't get paid. No money meant no **DEATH SQUADRON: APOCALYPSE** and with **ELLIE** wiping out all my savings on two dopey dolls I needed all the cash I could get. <u>I had to find that stupid cat.</u>

I went upstairs and made some 'WANTED' posters on my computer. Unfortunately the only photo I had of **Mr Yummy Whiskers** is the selfie he took of his bottom. Can you recognise a cat from his bottom? Who knows, but as it was the only photo I had, and you could just about see a bit of his face, I put it on the poster.

I spent the rest of the evening taping posters to lampposts and calling for **Mr Yummy Whiskers**. It was hard. I wanted to call loud enough so he'd hear me, but quiet enough so no one else would. Running up and down the street shouting 'Yummy Whiskers' at the top of your voice while sporting painted-on face fungus is a recipe for disaster. By the time I got home there was still no

sign. I was exhausted so I headed for bed.

As I was coming out of the bathroom Mum stopped me. She wanted to know why I was still wearing the cap even though I was in my pyjamas. I tried to think of a good reason, but she wasn't really listening. She was excited about something else. It turns out that **ELLIE** has done really well at school, so as a treat Mum and Dad had bought tickets to PRINCESS TWINKLE'S MAGIC CASTLE: LIVE! at the Arena Centre on Sunday. I laughed. It sounded <u>terrible</u>. But Mum wasn't finished. One of **ELLIE**'s friends was supposed to be going, but she had pulled out so now there was a spare ticket for me.

I just stood there shaking my head. There was no way I was going to watch

PRINCESS TWINKLE'S MAGIC CASTLE: LIVE!

Besides, on Sunday I was supposed to be queuing up for **DEATH SQUADRON: APOCALYPSE** and then playing it until my thumbs fell off. Mum wasn't listening, though. She said that it would be nice for **ELLIE** and me to 'spend some quality time together'. I told her that **ELLIE** was welcome to come and join me in the queue for **DEATH SQUADRON: APOCALYPSE** but apparently that wouldn't be 'appropriate', which we all know is mum-speak for 'We've got the tickets. You're coming.'

I adjusted my cap and stormed off to bed.

This day has been a total

I wish I hadn't blown my eyebrows off in science. How am I supposed to go on stage in front of everybody with no eyebrows? I should have paid more attention and then none of this would have happened. And as for **CLAUDIA**, I should have borrowed **JOSH**'s beard for the rehearsal today. If **CLAUDIA** likes **JOSH** in a beard, she'll love me! I can't really do anything about the PRINCESS TWINKLE'S MAGIC CASTLE: LIVE! show thing — Mum's bought the tickets and I can't change what someone else does. Besides, if I don't find Mr Yummy Whiskers soon I won't have the money for DEATH SQUADRON: APOCALYPSE anyway.

WEDNESDAY

When I woke up this morning I went straight to the bathroom to check on my eyebrows. They were back, sitting on my forehead like **two clever caterpillars**. I was so relieved I tried out all the expressions I'd missed yesterday:

1. Amused
2. Angry
3. Surprised
4. Just smelled a fart

All present and correct and all in perfect working order! It was good to have them back. I ran back into my bedroom and kissed my diary. **Thank you!**

It was only as I was heading into school that I noticed my chin was starting to get really itchy. It wasn't just my chin, either, my whole upper lip was twitching like a **body-popping pop tart**. I ran into the toilets to try and figure out what was happening. I had an angry rash all over the bottom half of my face. I looked like **JOSH** had looked. Then I remembered — the beard! I'd asked the diary to let me wear the beard yesterday to impress **CLAUDIA**. Big mistake! My face was coming out in **radioactive beard rash**.

As I looked in the mirror little white spots

started to appear. It was getting worse by the second. I looked like a plague victim. The bell rang — I was late so rushed to the classroom. I tried to keep my hand over my mouth so that no one would see but **BRAD RADLEY** noticed and punched me on the arm saying,

What's the matter, bozo boy? Bad breath?

The whole class started to laugh. But it soon got worse. When **BRAD** had nudged me I'd popped one of the spots and yellow gunk was seeping through my fingers.

Gross!

147

JOSH noticed first. He pointed at me and said

Yuck!

which we all know is Josh-speak for 'Look everyone, Fin's face is melting!' Soon I was the centre of attention and not in a good way. I looked like something out of a zombie movie. **CLAUDIA** looked like she was about to get sick. When Mrs Johnson saw what was going on she sent me to the school nurse.

This was a

I might have got my eyebrows back, but with only two days until HOT RODS' opening night my chin had exploded. The nurse took one look at my face and said 'Nasty!' Which we all know is nurse-speak for 'Amputate!' Just as I was thinking whether you could actually amputate someone's chin (and I wish you could — **BRAD RADLEY** and **JOSH DOYLE**, I'm looking at you) the nurse produced a vat of something and started to smear it all over my face with a lollipop stick.

IT WAS DISGUSTING! It looked like ice cream. It smelled like mayonnaise. Ugh. She plastered it all over me as if she was painting a garden wall. I had to sit in the nurse's office while the cream 'absorbed into my skin'. It took over an hour! I was so bored I offered to rearrange her pill bottle collection. When an hour was up she gave me some of the cream to take with me. I was supposed to put it on every other hour — no chance! It made me stink like a badger's bottom.

When I got back to class everyone turned to stare. I tried to cover my face with my hand again, but the cream was so sticky and squelchy, every time I touched it it made a disgusting sucking sound, like a pukey plughole. Mrs Johnson told me to stop fiddling or else it wouldn't get better. The smell was so bad nobody wanted to sit next to me. Mrs Johnson made me sit at the back near an open window. Even then, when the wind changed everyone coughed and spluttered. Try having it plastered TO YOUR CHIN, guys!

At break time, **CLIFF** and **JOSH** held their breath and ran over to talk to me. They tried to speak really quickly so they wouldn't have to breathe in while they were near me. They really, really, **REALLY** wanted me to join their band. They thought that if I listened to one of their songs I might really like it. I didn't know what I had to say to get through to them. I'd tried being polite so I decided to be rude instead! Maybe it was the fact that I had sat freezing my bottom off all morning, or maybe it was the fumes from my funky face-fungus cream, but I had had enough.

I told them System of the Future was the worst name ever for a band, that I would never join it and that they should stop asking.

In fact I told them **NEVER TO ASK ME AGAIN**. **JOSH** looked really hurt and I immediately felt bad, then I remembered it was his beard that had given me the rash and didn't feel so bad after all. **CLIFF** just looked like **CLIFF**, which was annoying in itself.

We spent all afternoon painting the set for HOT RODS. Mrs Johnson had found a load of pictures from olden times on the internet and was showing us what she wanted. There were loads of cool things to paint — a car, a diner, a funky skyline — but Mrs Johnson gave me a tin of red paint and a tiny paintbrush and told me to paint a wall. She thought it was probably best if I worked on my own as the smell might distract the other kids.

So while everyone else got to paint cool stuff, I stood at the back and painted a wall red. It was sooooo boring! After about two hours I wasn't even halfway through and I didn't have anyone to talk to. I decided my wall would look cooler if it had graffiti on it. I wasn't going to leave it on there for the play, I wasn't stupid! But I thought I could write funny things and then paint over them again without anyone noticing. I got a bit carried away. At first I just wrote 'Hey, bozo!' again and again and again. Then I started to write other things like:

WONKY MIKE
EATS DOG POO
ON SUNDAYS

CLIFF IS A
DWEEB

GUY TWO SAYS
MRS JOHNSON
CAN'T WRITE
PLAYS

Just as I was about to paint over everything Mrs Johnson came to check how I was doing. When she saw what I had written she blew her top! I've never seen her so angry. She said I had no respect for her 'artistic vision'. Even I don't know what that's teacher-speak for! I presume it's 'lousy play' but can't be sure. She took the paint off me and painted all over the graffiti herself, ranting and raving all the while. When she had finished she ordered me out of the theatre. I WAS OUT OF THE PLAY AGAIN.

When I got home I was about to put the face cream in the bin when Mum stopped me. The nurse had emailed home to let her know what had happened and to remind my mum to make sure I kept up the application. Mum took a fresh dollop of cream and splatted it on my face. I stank worse than ever.

At dinner Dad didn't eat a thing. He said the smell was so bad it was putting him off his food. Mum suggested I wear the cream morning, noon and night until Dad has lost a bit of weight. I think it was supposed to be a joke but neither Dad nor I found it very funny.

After dinner there was a knock on the door. It was our neighbour, Mr Scott. He had a load of **Mr Yummy Whiskers'** WANTED posters in his hand and he wasn't happy. He showed the posters to Mum and said that the image of a cat's backside plastered to every lamppost lowered the tone of the neighbourhood. He'd taken down the lot! I argued that you could actually see **Mr Yummy Whiskers'** face too, but Mum nudged me to make me stop talking and told Mr Scott she would make sure it didn't happen again. Just before Mr Scott left he sniffed.

What's that smell?

he said.

I wiggled my chin in his direction until he went away.

I was SOOOOO angry. All of my hard work had been for nothing. How was I supposed to find **Mr Yummy Whiskers** without my posters? Mum wasn't very sympathetic — she wondered how I was supposed to find **Mr Yummy Whiskers** with just a photo of his bum . . .

She dug out an old photo from ages ago and helped me make new posters. Just as I was about to go and put them outside Mum's tablet started to vibrate. It was Gran, she was video-calling from Tenerife. We all gathered around the screen to say hello. She said she was missing **Mr Yummy Whiskers** very much. She asked if she could see him right then and there. I panicked but Mum said he was out catching mice so couldn't come to the screen right now. Gran said never mind, it wasn't long till she was back on Saturday morning and she'd see him then.

Just as we were about to sign off Gran asked what was wrong with my face. I blamed a poor connection and made a crackling sound with my mouth. I got up to leave and she spotted the wanted posters in my hand. She was instantly suspicious — what were they for? I decided to lie and say it was a game I was playing with **ELLIE** — we'd made a load of joke posters that said 'Wanted for being the cutest cat in the world' and were putting them up around the house for a laugh. Amazingly Gran bought it and headed off for a 'siesta', which we all know is Gran-speak for 'cocktail'.

I spent the rest of the evening putting up posters — AGAIN — and smelling of toe cheese. I hope Mr Yummy Whiskers shows up by Saturday. It'll break Gran's heart if he doesn't. More importantly, I won't get my hands on her twenty pounds for DEATH SQUADRON: APOCALYPSE.

Now I'm sitting in bed writing this and stinking out my bedroom. I'm trying to think of the things I'd change today if I could. I can't change the beard rash, that happened yesterday. I <u>could</u> change the graffiti, but

I'm not sure I want to. Do I really want to be back in this play? I've been kicked out of it so many times, maybe it's just not meant to be. Perhaps I should have listened to my heart. My one stab at megastardom ended when I wet myself during the school Nativity. Maybe I'm just not meant to be on stage at all! But then I remember **CLIFF** and **CLAUDIA**, not to mention how angry Mrs Johnson was. Even if I don't want to be back in the play I can't have her angry at me for the rest of my life. I HAVE to change it.

So, diary, today I didn't paint any graffiti on the set of HOT RODS. I just painted a perfect red wall.

Time for bed. At least if I close my eyes the smell doesn't make them water . . .

THURSDAY

When I woke up this morning there was a big greasy stain on my pillow from the spot cream. It looked like a skating rink for slugs. Luckily the cream had worked its magic and my face was now spot free. I gave the pillow a good wipe and headed down for breakfast. There was still no sign of Mr Yummy Whiskers and Mum was starting to get worried. She had realised that while

I might have been *technically* in charge I was only twelve years old! She reckoned Gran might just be a teeny bit angry with her too.

Over breakfast she told us we were all going to have a look for the missing cat this evening. **ELLIE** hasn't put down her gENeRATiON CuTe dolls since she got them and they're really starting to annoy me. Every time she took a bite of toast she accidentally set one off. If there's one thing more annoying than eating scratching-post toast for breakfast, it's doing it while being forced to listen to 'SCHooL DANCe RoMANCe'.

At school, all anyone was talking about was the school play tomorrow. Everyone except **BRAD RADLEY** that is — he still wanted to talk about my exploding face. When I got to my desk I found a mask waiting for me. **BRAD** had drawn a skull and crossbones on it and written the word 'TOXIC' across the front. Very funny, **BRAD.**

Nobody mentioned anything about the graffiti incident yesterday and when Mrs Johnson came in she was smiling. Phew. She was really excited about her 'premiere' and couldn't believe that 'opening night' was tomorrow. Who does she think she is? Steven Spielberg? Everyone, apart from **JOSH DOYLE**, who already had his costume, had to go to a fitting at lunchtime with **JOSH DOYLE**'s mum.

I was pleased to be back in the play. It was nice to see everyone getting excited about something, and even though I only had one line I was still part of it. Even megastars have to start somewhere, right?

JOSH and **CLIFF** ignored me all first lesson. It was so childish! I IGNORED THEM RIGHT BACK! Just because they're new best friends and I don't want to be in their stupid band doesn't mean they can't speak to me. Although, I suppose I was quite rude to them yesterday. Maybe I should have asked the diary to fix it. Oh well, too late now.

Things got even worse when, at first break, **CLIFF** asked **CLAUDIA** to help him learn his lines. They both went off together to practise the last scene. I watched them from across the playground until **JOSH** saw me and said I was being a bit of a stalker. He's got a cheek! He's the one creeping up on people and accusing them of being stalkers! Then he went over to join the girls and all three of them started laughing and giggling. When Lisa, **CLAUDIA**'s friend, joined in it was too much for me to take.

I marched straight over and asked if they'd help me learn my lines too. **CLAUDIA** looked at me like I'd gone mad. She said, 'But you only have one line!', which we all know is Claudia-speak for 'Back off, loser!' I said my line anyway, and then when I was finished I looked a bit stupid just hanging around, so I pretended to study a particularly interesting tree. Way to go, Fin!

At lunchtime **JOSH** and **CLIFF** said they had an announcement to make. System of the Future had a song they wanted to play. Everyone was really excited (except me) and we all went down to Mr Burchester's music room to listen. I smiled, this was going to be terrible. They started playing this song called 'Loser Dude' and my face fell. I just knew it was about me! They'd written this horrible song about me and everyone was listening to it and nodding along! It went like this:

'He is so mean, He is so rude Nobody likes him Loser Dude!'

That was me! I was Loser Dude. As soon as the song finished I was so angry I couldn't

keep it in. I shouted,

That's me! I'm Loser Dude!

And it was only when people started to laugh that I realised what I'd done. I'd admitted to being a loser to everyone in my class. **BRAD RADLEY** sniggered and said, 'If you say so!' I tried to explain but no one was listening. **CLIFF** said the song wasn't about 'anyone in particular'. Which we all know is Cliff-speak for 'In your face, Loser Dude!'

Afterwards I went to the canteen and had some lunch. It was spaghetti Bolognese and it looked like an explosion in a worm farm. What with that and the song, I was really angry by the time I finally got outside to play. **JOSH** and a few people were playing football. I went to join in. I made sure I was on the opposite team to **JOSH** so I could give him a lesson in proper football. Have you ever had one of those games where everything you do works out perfectly? I have and it was today. I scored three goals and by the time I'd finished, if anyone looked like a Loser Dude it was **JOSH**.

As I was finishing my second victory lap, one of the other kids asked why I hadn't been to have my costume fitting yet. My blood ran cold. It was only then that I noticed the people who were playing football weren't acting in the play apart from **JOSH**, who had already got his costume. He winked at me. He'd done it on purpose! WHO WAS THE LOSER DUDE NOW?

I ran to the empty classroom Mrs Doyle was using as a fitting room. When I got there she was already packing away. She thought she'd seen everybody. She didn't even know there was a Guy Two. What was she talking about? DIDN'T SHE KNOW SHE WAS DEALING WITH A MEGASTAR HERE? Without me there is no play! She said she only had a couple of bits and pieces left so she made me put them on.

I looked ridiculous. I had a bandana and a pair of shorts so tight they cut off my circulation. Then she gave me a vest that was supposed to show off my muscles. Instead it made me look punier than ever. Just when

I thought things couldn't get any worse she produced a pair of trainers that were at least five sizes too big for me. She said if I tied the laces really tight they should be fine. I looked at myself in the mirror. NOTHING WAS EVER GOING TO MAKE THIS FINE.

After lunch Mrs Johnson asked everyone to put on their costumes for a dress rehearsal. I thought about refusing, but I didn't want to get kicked out of the school play again. Everyone else looked really cool. Especially **CLIFF**. He had this ace leather jacket and a pair of shades; he looked like a member of **X-WING**. I looked like I shopped blindfolded in a charity shop. I tried to think of a way to make my outfit look just a little bit cooler. I remembered the 'toxic' mask and pulled it on. I thought it made me look amazing. Mrs Johnson disagreed. Apparently Guy Two 'would never wear a mask.' I pointed out that Guy Two probably wouldn't wear hot pants and a string vest either, but she wasn't listening.

As we were walking out to get changed back into our uniforms I tripped over my size ridiculous shoes and tumbled into the desk. This costume was dangerous! If I'd got to the costume fitting earlier maybe I would have got a better outfit. Well, that's something I *can* fix.

COME ON, DIARY –

tomorrow make it so that I got to the fitting first and had the pick of all the clothes.

By the time I got home Mum was already out looking for **Mr Yummy Whiskers**. Dad and **ELLIE** had gone down one side of the street so she and I walked down the other.

BRAD RADLEY saw me and called over, 'Out for a walk with your mum, Fin?' That was bad enough, but then Mum started shouting 'Mr Yummy Whiskers!' at the top of her voice. When he heard this, **BRAD** laughed so hard his face went purple.

We knocked on doors, asked people to check in sheds, looked in bins and went all the way around the block. There was no sign of the cat at all. Mum seemed worried. I'm starting to think **Mr Yummy Whiskers** may have gone to visit the great cat flap in the sky. WHAT AM I GOING TO TELL GRAN?

FRIDAY

When I woke up I'd forgotten all about **Mr Yummy Whiskers**. This was the day all of humanity was waiting for. This was the day **FIN SPENCER** became a megastar! If the diary had worked I'd even have the megastar costume to match! Sure, I may only have one line, and I'm still not sure what a bozo is for . . .

— but I wasn't going to let that stop me! I'd decided not to tell Mum, Dad and **ELLIE** about the play until after opening night. There were two chances to see it and I wanted to make sure it wasn't going to be completely awful before standing in front of my family — particularly **ELLIE** — and making a fool of myself. Besides if **ELLIE** came she'd probably bring those two ɠeNeRATіᴼN (Ute dolls with her. It'd be really distracting to have them going off every five minutes. This megastar needs to focus!

Unfortunately, things didn't go

according to plan. In fact, this megastar is in more trouble than he's ever been in in his life . . .

Mrs Johnson had given the whole day over to getting ready for the big show. All of the costumes were lined up in the classroom and my diary had worked its magic once more. There, on a hanger with my name stuck to the top, were THE COOLEST CLOTHES I HAD EVER SEEN. Mrs Doyle had really outdone herself! I had a pair of ripped jeans, a black leather jacket and some shades that made Guy Two look like Guy Two Million. It was only as I was pulling on my outfit that I noticed the clown-size shoes I'd worn yesterday. They still had my name in them. Well, at least the diary had got it half right.

Besides, when you looked that cool all over, who was going to notice your shoes?

Mrs Johnson called a dress rehearsal in the theatre and everything was going fine until the fight scene between Guy Two and Sebastian. I'd been looking forward to this. Anything that gave me the chance to beat up **CLIFF**, even if we were only pretending, was something worth looking forward to. It all started well. I swung my first punch and blocked his kick. Then I was supposed to lean in and pretend to punch him on the nose. I was supposed to stop short and miss, only **something went wrong**.

As I was leaning in, I tripped over my ridiculous shoes and didn't stop short at all. My fist kept on going and it really did punch

CLIFF on the nose. I felt it crunch and everything. **CLIFF** let out this huge cry and collapsed, clutching his face. Blood was pouring from between his fingers. This looked bad. THIS LOOKED VERY BAD INDEED. It didn't help that **CLIFF** was rolling around on the floor like an Italian footballer. I hadn't hit him that hard and besides, it had been an accident.

Nobody else seemed to see it like that.

The school nurse was called and then **CLIFF** was sent to hospital in an ambulance. Apparently it looked like his nose might have been broken.

When everyone came back into the theatre I wasn't very popular. I tried to explain what had happened, pointing at my feet and blaming the shoes. I said that if this was anybody's fault it was **JOSH DOYLE'S** mum's. **JOSH** didn't like that! He said I'd had it in for **CLIFF** from day one and this was probably revenge for the song I thought they'd written about me.

Things were looking bad. No **CLIFF** meant no Sebastian and no Sebastian meant no play and no opening night. Whether I'd meant it or not, I'd ruined this for everyone. Only Mrs Johnson was still smiling. She calmed everyone down and said that 'everything was going to be all right.' WHAT WAS SHE TALKING ABOUT? Her leading man was in hospital, everything was **NOT** going to be all right!

Then she turned to me. Apparently everything was going to be all right because **CLIFF** had an understudy.

Fin Spencer was going to save the day. I _had_ learned the lines, right?

My heart began to beat like a monkey in a drum shop. This was bad, this was very bad. OF COURSE I HADN'T LEARNED ALL THE LINES! Did she think I had nothing better to do with my time? I had a psychotic cat to find, I'd been at a hippy health retreat and I had **ELLIE**'s gENeRAT?ON (ute dolls to deal with, for goodness' sake! Not to mention school! WHEN DID SHE THINK I HAD TIME TO LEARN LINES I THOUGHT I'D NEVER NEED TO SAY?

I didn't say any of this, of course. I just smiled and played for time. What was I going to do? Everyone was looking at me. I'd ruined the play for everyone and put a really popular kid in hospital. If I told them I didn't know the lines then I might as well emigrate to Antarctica and become a penguin.

Besides, I *kind of* knew the lines. I'd read the script once *and* I'd been at every rehearsal. I'd seen everybody do everything, I was sure some of it must have gone in.

And there was something else very important to consider. Now that I was Sebastian I finally got to kiss **CLAUDIA RONSON**. What choice did I have? Admit I hadn't learned the lines and ruin everything for everyone or end up kissing **CLAUDIA RONSON** live on stage. It was no choice at all!

I smiled and said as confidently as I could,

Of course I know all the lines, Miss!

Which we all know is Fin-speak for, 'Help!' Mrs Johnson nodded and said,

That's settled then.

It couldn't be that hard, right?

WRONG!

The opening night of HOT RODS was forty-five minutes of my life that I want to erase from my memory with a nuclear bomb. I didn't know the songs. I didn't know the lines. The only one I got right was 'Hey, bozo!' which wasn't a line my character said any more. At one point I stood on the stage and had absolutely no idea what I was supposed to say so I told one of my jokes.

What do you get if you cross someone called Rodney with a BBQ? A hot rod!

Nobody laughed.

In the body-popping sequence I trod on **JOSH**'s toes and knocked away his walking stick. He fell off the stage, his beard pinged off and hit Mr Finch in the eye. By the time we got to the love duet at the end I was kind of relieved that the play was nearly over and terrified because it was the song I knew least well. . .

CLAUDIA sang one line to me and I was supposed to sing the next line back to her. I figured that as long as I was quick enough to think of something that rhymed with whatever she said, no one would even notice if they weren't the right words. Unfortunately some of the rhymes were really hard. I did my best to keep up and it all started out OK . . .

Claudia: I love the way you give me advice

Fin: I think your teeth are really, really nice...

Sure 'nice teeth' is a bit of an odd thing to say, but I got away with it.

Unfortunately I didn't get away with it for long.

Claudia: I love the way you always say please.

Fin: I think you smell like a really nice cheese...

OOPS. No girl wants to be told they smell like cheese. Not even a really nice one. By the time we got to the last line I was panicking. I don't even know what made me say it. . .

Claudia: I love the way you'll be mine forever.

Fin: I think your eyes are too close together . . .

The whole audience gasped and **CLAUDIA**'s bottom lip started to tremble. At that point in the song I was supposed to lean in for a kiss. I did my best but **CLAUDIA** was already running from the stage in floods of tears. Mrs Johnson pulled down the curtain and the world premiere of HOT RODS was over.

I didn't know what to do. Everyone was staring at me. There was no applause. In fact, the audience were booing. I didn't think you were allowed to boo at school plays. SURELY THERE'S A RULE AGAINST IT SOMEWHERE? I'd never seen Mrs Johnson so angry. Luckily it was that type of angry where nobody says anything. They just stand there and quiver for a bit while smoke comes out of their ears.

I used the silence to make my escape. I ran as fast as my silly shoes would let me and didn't look back.

When I got home I came straight upstairs and checked the diary. This was all the fault of my size one million shoes.

WHY HADN'T THE DIARY FIXED IT?

When I checked what I'd written I realised
I'd only asked it to change my clothes. I'd
said nothing about shoes. You'd have thought
the diary would know what I meant, but I'm
starting to remember how this diary has a
habit of backfiring on me . . .

But it doesn't matter. I CAN STILL USE THE DIARY TO FIX WHAT JUST HAPPENED. If I hadn't rehearsed the fight sequence with **CLIFF** in the dress rehearsal then I wouldn't have bopped him on the nose, he'd have still been in the play and I wouldn't have made a fool of myself in front of everyone. So I just need not to have hit **CLIFF**. But . . .

I've had an even better idea! What if I still bop **CLIFF** on the nose, only I've also learned all the lines and dance moves like I was supposed to? Then I would still have been leading man, only this time I'll have saved the play *and* kissed **CLAUDIA RONSON**.

So, diary, that's what I want you to make happen. Are you listening? To make up for the shoe thing, you're going to fix it so that this morning I got up really early, learned all the lines and dance moves and then I saved the play.

WORK FOR ME, DIARY.

Megastardom awaits.

SATURDAY

This morning I got into the shower and, as I was trying to decide whether I wanted to smell of Sunblushed Sunsets or Blueberry Bubbles, I started to sing 'You and Me Always', the duet from HOT RODS. And not the **FIN SPENCER** version either, the right version, with all the right words in the right order. It was only as I was scrubbing myself dry with a towel smaller than an ant's kilt, that I realised what this meant. If I knew the words to 'You and Me Always' this morning when I didn't last night,

THEN THE DIARY MUST HAVE WORKED!

While I was getting dressed I mentally ran through all of Sebastian's lines. I knew every single one! Then I tried some of the dance moves I was supposed to know. I knew those too. I was so excited I body-popped into the kitchen. Mum thought I was having a fit and wanted to call the doctor. **Charming!** My parents wouldn't know a cool dance if they found Michael

Jackson moonwalking in the fridge. When I explained all about the body-popping and the play she immediately wanted to come and see it tonight. **Megastars have that effect on people . . .**

If my calculations were correct, last night I became the Channing Tatum of our school and saved the day. Tonight I was going to do it all again. It would be good for my family to witness my first steps on the road to megastardom.

After breakfast Mum got on the computer and emailed Mrs Johnson for three tickets. There was also an email from Gran. She'd decided to extend her holiday until Monday. Result! That meant I still had a couple of days to find Mr Yummy Whiskers.

I felt so good I body-popped out of the kitchen and headed for the shops. I needed a bag of crisps. The table-leg toast wasn't the right kind of breakfast for a megastar. I wasn't sure prawn cocktail flavour crisps would be either but they didn't sell caviar.

As I was coming out of the shop I bumped in to CLAUDIA's friend Lisa. She congratulated me on being brilliant in the school play last night. **Apparently I'd really stolen the show.** She had no idea I could act and dance and sing like that. To be honest, neither did I and quite frankly I couldn't until the diary had worked its magic! I was so pleased my brain did a little back flip.

As I tucked into my crisps I thought about how perfectly everything had turned out. Last night I became an ace actor, I kissed **CLAUDIA RONSON** in front of everybody and my whole school thinks I'm some kind of hero. Well, maybe not the WHOLE school. **CLIFF SHRAPNEL** probably thinks I'm a bit of a bumblehead for punching him on the nose and putting him in hospital. I feel a little bit bad about that, but you know, nobody said becoming a megastar was easy. Sacrifices have to be made, even if they're by someone else. Thank you, **CLIFF SHRAPNEL**.

I gave Lisa an autograph, even though she didn't ask for one, and headed for home. This megastar needed to rest — or at least play **DEATH SQUADRON** all day — until his second big performance. The whole school was depending on me.

That evening, I headed to school for the big night. From backstage I peeked between the curtains and saw Mum, Dad and **ELLIE** sitting on the front row. Perfect! I was going to blow their socks off. I headed into my dressing room — Classroom 7B — expecting a hero's welcome. But when I walked through the door I realised the hero's welcome had already been given to someone else.

There, sitting in Mrs Johnson's comfy chair, surrounded by people patting him on the back, was **CLIFF SHRAPNEL**. He had a little bit of tape over his nose but apart from that he was fine! What did I tell you — I knew I'd barely touched him! He is such a CRY-BABY! In fact, I bet he made me hit him on purpose to get me in trouble. **JOSH** was actually giving him a shoulder massage! It looked like **CLIFF SHRAPNEL** was back.

But to my horror, not only was he back but he was **BACK IN THE PLAY!**

Mrs Johnson made a little speech about

how she knew she was right to make **CLIFF** the star of the show. She could tell from the way he'd soldiered on in the first audition that he was the leading man for her and nothing would stop him carrying on with the show. I was demoted back to Guy Two and **CLIFF** was centre stage once more. As we got into costume **CLIFF** came over, patted me on the back and said,

No hard feelings.

Which we all know is Cliff Speak for 'In your face, Loser Dude!'

As I waited for my cue to go onstage I listened to **CLIFF** deliver all his lines and get the laughter and applause that should have been mine. Even when I did get to strut my megastar stuff, the fight scene wasn't very good. **CLIFF** was so scared I'd punch him again he kept ducking out of the way before I even pretended to hit him.

THIS WAS SO UNFAIR! Last night I'd had the night of my life but I couldn't remember any of it. Tonight, when I was there to remember it, the only line I got to say was 'Hey, bozo!'

Last night I finally got to kiss **CLAUDIA RONSON** and everybody remembered it but me. Tonight, I got to watch **CLAUDIA RONSON** kiss someone else and I'll remember it always. I'm starting to remember why I stopped using this diary. **WHAT'S THE POINT IN BEING FINCREDIBLE IF YOU DON'T REMEMBER A THING?**

Mum and Dad could see I was disappointed and did their best to cheer me up. They said I said my one line very well. **ELLIE** wanted to know what a bozo was . . .

WHAT IS A BOZO?

A) AN EGYPTIAN GOD
B) A GOLF SWING
C) A CHINESE COMIC BOOK

WHO KNOWS!?!

Unfortunately nothing anyone could say would make it better. It wasn't like there was another chance tomorrow to put things right.

Tonight had been the final performance of HOT RODS.

As if that wasn't bad enough, for the rest of the evening **ELLIE** kept saying 'bozo this' and 'bozo that'. When she wanted some ketchup for her fish and chips it was 'Hey, bozo! Pass the ketchup!' When I changed the channel on the remote it was, 'Hey, bozo! I was watching that!'

Brilliant. Thanks to Mrs Johnson, I'm going to be a bozo forever and I still don't know what it means!

SUNDAY

Today should have been amazing. My plan had been to stand all morning in the queue to get **DEATH SQUADRON: Apocalypse** and then spend the rest of the day sitting in my room playing it until my thumbs were two worn-out stumps. It was a simple enough plan, so why did it go so wrong?

Well, first of all Gran's extended holiday meant I hadn't got my twenty pounds. To be honest I may never get that twenty-pound note if **Mr Yummy Whiskers** doesn't show up soon. **ELLIE** had wiped out the rest of the cash I needed by buying two ꒱ꪖ𝖓ꫀꪖꪖꪻꪖ꒐ꪮꪀ Cute dolls, so I didn't have enough anyway. It was a disaster. The other thing that happened was PRinCeSS TWINKle'S MaGiC CaStle: LiVe!

The only queue I got to stand in today was the one full of six-year-old girls in sparkly princess outfits as we waited to be let into the Arena Centre. **ELLIE** was so excited she'd even bought her ꒱ꪖ𝖓ꫀꪖꪖꪻꪖ꒐ꪮꪀ Cute dolls with her so they could enjoy it too. To be fair, the only way you could possibly enjoy PRinCeSS TWINKle'S MaGiC CaStle:

LIVE! was if you were a twelve-inch-high plastic doll. Or a six-year-old girl. Both seem to have the same taste.

PRINCESS TWINKLE'S MAGIC CASTLE: LIVE! made HOT RODS look like Shakespeare. It was all about PRINCESS TWINKLE and her best friend Fluffy Cloud. They had to go on an adventure into space to rescue a rainbow from a fish. I had no idea why. As if that wasn't bad enough, every five minutes they showered the audience with glitter. It was like being trapped in a fancy dress shop with a crazy clown. It made my eyes hurt, and when they started singing it made my ears hurt too! They sang sooooo many terrible songs:

A Rainbow's Just a Smile Upside Down
Don't Touch the Tiara
The Castle Cupcake Hoedown

Dad thought that the interval was the end of the show and was already halfway to the car when Mum stopped him. When she explained that we had to sit through the same again he went very quiet, took out his wallet and joined the queue for the sweetie stand. He came back with more sweets than I have ever seen. Looks like the diet's off. **Good to have you back, Dad!**

The second half was made more bearable by the sweets, but by the time we reached the final number, 'Rainbows are Everywhere', I was more than ready to go home. Unfortunately PRINCESS TWINKLE had a sting in her tiara. When everybody thought the show was over, it hadn't really ended because PRINCESS TWINKLE had a surprise for us. I dreaded to think what that twelve-foot fluffy pink maniac might think of as a surprise. **I DIDN'T HAVE TO WAIT LONG TO FIND OUT.** Suddenly everything went dark and when the lights came back on GENERATION CUTE were standing on the stage and the place was going wild.

ELLIE stood up on her seat and waved her two dolls in the air. She struggled to stay balanced so gave one of them to me to hold — 'Here you are, bozo!' I thought about catapulting her off the chair and into the ceiling but Mum would probably tell me off. I wasn't sure about Dad — at that moment he might actually have let me get away with it!

GENERATION CUTE were there to sing their new single 'HEART TWIRL GIRL' and, what was more, they wanted some kids from the audience to join them onstage. What kind of loser would want to join GENERATION CUTE onstage?

Well, every six-year-old girl on the planet, apparently.

PRINCESS TWINKLE'S fairy helpers came out into the audience looking for people to pick. ELLIE waved her doll like crazy in the air as they passed and they came and grabbed her. When they saw me holding **ELLIE**'s other doll they thought I must be a superfan AND GRABBED ME TOO!

I tried to stop them, but it's really hard to stop a fairy helper and if you punch them it looks bad. I called for Dad to help but he just grinned, shook his head and kept on eating his sweets. As far as he was concerned this was the best thing to happen all afternoon!

Soon I was up onstage in front of everybody, along with three six-year-old girls, all of ꒒ENERATION CUTE and a dancing rainbow. Kill me. **Kill me now!** Even writing about it is making me cringe. ꒒ENERATION CUTE started to sing and their new song is really bad:

'You're my heart twirl girl,
You've got my heart in a whirl!
You make my eyes swirl,
I love you, heart twirl girl!'

But the crowd are going crazy and then **ELLIE** and the other girls start to dance. They're terrible. Of course they're terrible. They're six. I'm the only person on stage who isn't six, in a boyband or a rainbow covered in glitter. At first I refuse to join in. I stand there with my arms folded. I want to crawl into a hole.

But then I see that, even though they're awful, the crowd are going wild for the kids' dancing. I wonder how the crowd would react if they saw some real dancing, so I start to jig along. The crowd cheer. Then I remember, thanks to the diary, that I know all the dance moves from HOT RODS. I try some of them out and the crowd start to cheer and clap even louder. Before I know it, I'M ACTUALLY STARTING TO ENJOY THIS.

Then Harold or Sebastian or whoever he is starts to rap, and I do a bit of **CLIFF**'s body-popping. By now the other kids have stopped to watch and someone's put a spotlight on me. I body-pop as hard as I can. The crowd go wild and I do some more. Then the other four members of GENERATiON CUTE come over and I'm showing them how to do it. By the end of the song, I'm standing with GENERATiON CUTE and they're all body-popping along with me! I start to smile. This is actually brilliant!

When the song finishes GENERATiON CUTE strike a pose and I'm there in the middle of them. Everybody is taking photographs, and I am grinning from ear to ear. So this is what it really feels like to be a **MEGASTAR!**

When I get back to my seat the audience is still clapping and cheering. Even **ELLIE** is smiling, and whenever anybody asks she tells them proudly, 'That's my brother!' Dad offers me a Caramel Swirl, and Mum is really pleased I 'joined in', which is mum-speak for 'Way to go Fin!' As we make our way back to the car I keep getting stopped. I pose for photos, do a little bit of body-popping and even sign a few autographs — this time because people actually ask me to!

When we get home I am still grinning from ear to ear. But when I see **Mr Yummy Whiskers'** food bowl I stop grinning. There's still no sign of the mangy cat and Gran's definitely back tomorrow. She'll kill me when she finds out, megastar or not! I persuade Mum and Dad to come outside for one last look around the block. **ELLIE** reluctantly says she'll come too so long as she can bring her ꒓ENERATꙆON ꓛUTE dolls. I don't mind — the more people looking for this cat the better, even if two of them are plastic.

We walk around the block calling for **Mr Yummy Whiskers** but there's still no sign. As we're about to head for home **ELLIE** accidentally sets off one of her ꒓ENERATꙆON ꓛUTE dolls. Just as he finishes singing I hear a little 'meow' coming from somewhere. It's **Mr Yummy Whiskers**, but where is he? Then I remember, the sound of those dolls sends him wild! I tell **ELLIE** to squeeze them again, then I grab the other one and squeeze it too. The louder Harold or Sebastian or whoever squawks the louder **Mr Yummy Whiskers'** meows get!

We follow the noise and just as we get back to our house **ELLIE** and I squeeze the dolls together one last time and a tired, dirty and very cold **Mr Yummy Whiskers** jumps out from under a bush and into our arms. He stinks, he's filthy and he's made my life a misery but I cuddle him anyway.

When we get **Mr Yummy Whiskers** home we have to give him some food and a bath.

He's so angry I think he might run away again. I make a bed for him in my uniform drawer — taking my uniform out first, of course! — to make sure he'll stay put tonight and head for bed, listening to the gentle purring snores of one very happy cat. Despite not getting to play **DEATH SQUADRON: APOCALYPSE** there's nothing I'd change about today. Who knew a trip to watch **PRINCESS TWINKLE** would be perfect? Maybe **ELLIE**'s onto something. <u>NEVER</u> tell her I said that!

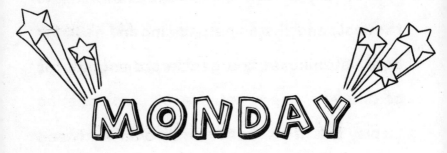

MONDAY

This morning the Coco Snaps were back on the table and the diet was over — result! It was going to be a good day. What's more **Mr Yummy Whiskers** was still in my uniform drawer so Gran should be very happy when she comes over after school to collect him. As we were eating breakfast Dad turned on the news and I almost asked him to switch over when the news report started to talk about a 'very special guest appearance' at the Mega Arena yesterday. OK, so GENERATION CUTE were cooler than I thought, and they'd helped find **Mr Yummy Whiskers**, kind of, but I'd heard enough for now!

But the news report wasn't about them. Well, it was, but GENERATION CUTE weren't the special guest stars t̶ talking about. As we watched, some s̶ camera-phone footage of me teaching GENERATION CUTE how to body-pop appeared on the screen. I couldn't believe it! The news report talked about a

'mystery body-popping megastar who had stolen the show!'

Apparently, the footage had gone viral and people everywhere were talking about it, even in America. I began to smile. This was good. This was very good indeed!

When I got to school it turned out lots of people had seen the news report that morning and I was a bit of a hero. **BRAD RADLEY** even asked me to autograph his forehead ~~h~~ saw what I was about to do ~~'~~wouldn't be appropriate'. Which ~~is~~ teacher-speak for 'I want to thing!'

But the truth was, nothing could ruin the day I was having. It got even better when **CLIFF**, **JOSH** and **CLAUDIA** found me before class. **CLAUDIA** asked me out! CAN YOU BELIEVE IT?! She said it would be like

they were haky

going out with a member of GENERATION CUTE! I was a bit confused — didn't she want to go out with **CLIFF**? **CLIFF** laughed. Apparently he already had a girlfriend at the school he used to be at — he wasn't interested in **CLAUDIA** at all.

RESULT!

CLAUDIA and I are going on date two next Saturday, so long as I don't kill another spider or anything. She suggested the burger bar again, but I reckon we should go for pizza. You can't choke on a pizza, can you?

Once my date with **CLAUDIA** was in the diary, **CLIFF** and **JOSH** asked if I would seriously reconsider joining their band. Apparently it didn't have to be called System of the Future if I didn't want it to be. It could be called anything. They needed a body-popping viral megastar in the group. I agreed to join. If it hadn't been for **CLIFF**'s body-popping I wouldn't even be a megastar, and now I know he's not trying to ruin my life completely, I think we could be friends. It'd be nice to see **JOSH** a bit more too. Even though I never thought I'd say it, I miss him. Besides, the name System of the Future has started to grow on me . . .

To seal the deal **CLIFF** invited me over to play **DEATH SQUADRON: APOCALYPSE** after school. His Dad had bought him a copy to make up for him missing the opening night of HOT RODS. As that was technically my fault, he thought I should come and enjoy it too. **CLIFF**, **JOSH** and I all shook hands. Playing rock music and playing **DEATH SQUADRON**: Apocalypse? THESE GUYS SOUNDED LIKE MY KIND OF PEOPLE!

When I got home Gran was waiting for me, cuddling **Mr Yummy Whiskers**. She gave me another massive box of chocolates. Now that Dad was off his health kick I got to enjoy them immediately too. As she was leaving she handed me a twenty-pound note and told me she was planning a SIX-MONTH round the world cruise next year, and would I be interested in looking after **Mr Yummy Whiskers**? I gulped. I wasn't really sure what to say when thankfully Mum answered for me. 'We'll think about it!' she said. Which we all know is mum-speak for 'Absolutely no way!'

As Gran was clambering into her car **ELLIE** rushed down with a present for **Mr Yummy Whiskers**. It was one of her ᵍeNeʀATᵢᵒN ᶜUᵗe dolls, Harold or Sebastian or whoever. She'd gone right off ᵍeNeʀATᵢᵒN ᶜUᵗe overnight. Apparently when your big brother is cooler than all of them, they lose some of their appeal.

After Gran left we headed for bed and I asked **ELLIE** what she was going to do with the other ᵍeNeʀATᵢᵒN ᶜUᵗe doll. She said that she didn't know so I asked if I could have it. **ELLIE** was happy to hand it over. I put it on my bookcase to remind me of today. Maybe ᵍeNeʀATᵢᵒN ᶜUᵗe weren't so bad. They'd turned me into a **megastar**, after all.

As for this diary, I think it might be time to put it away again. It causes more trouble than it solves, and once you start using it it's really hard to stop. So this is definitely

THE LAST ENTRY.

Besides, megastars don't need magic diaries! Everything they want just happens magically anyway, right? So, this is

FIN SPENCER: MEGASTAR

signing off.

Now, where did I leave my sunglasses? Watch out, bozo! **Megastar coming through!**